POINTS
of
DEPARTURE

NEW STORIES
FROM MEXICO

EDITED by MÓNICA LAVÍN

Translated by Gustavo V. Segade

CITY LIGHTS
SAN FRANCISCO

Cover design: Rex Ray
Book design: Elaine Katzenberger
Typography: Harvest Graphics

 This book was made possible by a grant from the Mexico/U.S. Fund for Culture and the institutions that support it: the Rockefeller Foundation, Fundación Cultural Bancomer, and Fondo Nacional para la Cultura y las Artes.

Library of Congress Cataloging-in-Publication Data

    Points of departure : new stories from Mexico / edited by Mónica Lavín ; translated by Gustavo Segade.
        p.   cm.
    ISBN 0-87286-381-6
    1. Short stories, Mexican—Translations into English.   2. Mexican fiction—20th century—Translations into English.   I. Lavín, Mónica, 1955–   ii. Segade, Gustavo Valentín, 1936–
PQ7288.E8 P65 2001
863'.0108972'09049—dc21

                                        00-065636
                                         CIP

Visit our website: www.citylights.com

CITY LIGHTS BOOKS are edited by Lawrence Ferlinghetti and Nancy J. Peters and published at the City Lights Bookstore, 261 Columbus Avenue, San Francisco, CA 94133

ACKNOWLEDGMENTS

"La vida real [Real Life]" by Eduardo Antonio Parra was published in the collection *Tierra de nadie* (México: Ediciones Era, 1999).

"Reina de sombras [Queen of Shadows]" by Bernardo Ruíz was published in *La sangre de tu corazón* (México: Universidad Nacional Autónoma de México, 1999).

"Junio le dio la voz [June Gave Him the Voice]" by Josefina Estrada was published in *Malagato* (México: Plaza y Valdés, 1990).

"Llamadas nocturnas [Night Calls]" by Rafael Pérez Gay appeared in *Llamadas nocturnas* (México: Cal y Arena, 1993).

"No cedería el lugar [He Wouldn't Give Up His Turn]" by Humberto Rivas was included in the collection *Los abrazos caníbales* (México: Océano, 1998).

"El basilisco [The Basilisk]" by Daniel Sada appeared in *El límite* (México; Vuelta, 1997).

"SchehereSade" by Rosa Beltrán was first published in *La Jornada Semanal de La Jornada*, February 20, 2000.

"La brocha gorda {The Big Brush]" by David Toscana appeared in *Historias del Lontanaza* (México: Planeta, 1998).

"Coyote" by Juan Villoro was published in *La casa pierde* (México: Alfaguara, 1998).

"A qué volver? [Why Come Back?]" by Mónica Lavín appeared in the collection *Ruby Tuesday no ha muerto* (México: Diana, 1998).

"La corbata de Ginsberg [Ginsberg's Tie]" by Juvenal Acosta was published in *sábado de unomásuno*, December 12, 1999.

"El rehén [The Hostage]" by Álvaro Uribe appeared in *La linterna de los muertos* (México: Fondo de Cultura Económica, 1998).

"Morente" by Rosina Conde was published in *Embotellado de origen* (México: Consejo Nacional para la Cultura y las Artes-Instituto Cultural de Sinaloa, 1994).

"Olga o el más oscuro mambo [Olga, or The Darkest Mambo]" by Mauricio Montiel was published in *Insomnios del otro lado* (México: Joaquín Mortiz, 1994).

"Isaías VII, 14 [Isaiah VII, 14]" by Ethel Krauze appeared in *El lunes te amaré* (México, Oceáno, 1987).

"Amor propio [Self-Love]" by Enrique Serna appeared in the collection *Amores de segunda mano* (México: Cal y Arena, 1994).

"Marina Dosal, aguafresquera [Marina Dosal, Juice Vendor]" by Francisco Hinojosa appeared in *Cuentos héticos* (México: Joaquín Mortiz, 1996).

EDITOR'S ACKNOWLEDGMENTS

My deepest thanks to Gustavo V. Segade, who I first met as the translator of one of my stories and who devoted a great deal of time to this book, translating the stories with enormous patience throughout all of the changes and revised decisions. His experience and sense of humor honor us.

Jaime Erasto Cortés, professor at the Universidad Nacional Autónoma de México and a specialist in the Mexican short story, was an invaluable guide and aide in choosing the authors and stories to be included, helping me to discern the criteria for an anthology such as this one, and discussing the translations with Gustavo. I was a grateful apprentice under his literary expertise.

The Mexico/U.S. Fund for Culture generously supported this project with a grant that made this most exciting quest possible.

Last but not least, my gratitude to City Lights editor Elaine Katzenberger for her dedicated labor in refining the selections and the translations, for her enthusiasm for this project from the outset, and for her detailed care in the making of the book. Gambling together on this collection of stories was a rewarding adventure. I would like to make a special mention of my friend Juvenal Acosta who, under the blue skies of San Francisco over a meal at Enrico's on Columbus Avenue, introduced me to Elaine and talked me into this project. What was then an enthusiastic conversation has now become a book.

And many thanks, of course, to City Lights, a prestigious house with a tradition of publishing literature from all over the world, which is now a home for my colleagues and me. We are delighted.

CONTENTS

INTRODUCTION   ix

REAL LIFE   1
   Eduardo Antonio Parra

QUEEN OF SHADOWS   15
   Bernardo Ruíz

JUNE GAVE HIM THE VOICE   29
   Josefina Estrada

NIGHT CALLS   37
   Rafael Pérez Gay

HE WOULDN'T GIVE UP HIS TURN   45
   Humberto Rivas

THE BASILISK   49
   Daniel Sada

SCHEHERESADE   57
   Rosa Beltrán

THE BIG BRUSH   65
   David Toscana

COYOTE   77
   Juan Villoro

WHY COME BACK? 93
Mónica Lavín

GINSBERG'S TIE 97
Juvenal Acosta

THE HOSTAGE 107
Álvaro Uribe

MORENTE 119
Rosina Conde

OLGA, OR THE DARKEST MAMBO 127
Mauricio Montiel

ISAIAH VII, 14 133
Ethel Krauze

SELF-LOVE 143
Enrique Serna

MARINA DOSAL, JUICE VENDOR 151
Francisco Hinojosa

Introduction

IF WRITING IS AN ADVENTURE, THEN SELECTING THE STORIES TO CREATE A representative sample of the work of contemporary Mexican authors is twice that because of the risks it presents and the awe it inspires. *Points of Departure* brings together seventeen outstanding short stories by Mexican writers born in the 1950s and 1960s. Though I am much more accustomed to the roles of writer and reader, I set out to construct this book motivated by curiosity, by loyalty to the genre, and by the desire to create a space for my colleagues to be published in the United States.

What you have in your hands is not only a sampling of recent writing by noteworthy Mexican authors, but also the result of an enthusiastic and dedicated team working at a long distance. When I first began this project, I enlisted the aid of Jaime Erasto Cortés, professor at the Universidad Nacional Autónoma de México, a specialist in the Mexican short story and one of the few devoted to the study of contemporary authors working in that genre. He acted as my primary consultant in the initial selection of authors and works, and many of the short stories presented here were chosen through our painstaking collaboration. Gustavo Segade, who patiently and enthusiastically translated all of the stories, also participated in these preliminary discussions via e-mail, fax, the telephone, and conventional mail. Finally, Elaine Katzenberger, my editor at City Lights, reflected on the choice of texts to create the most attractive mosaic possible. Our goal was to put together a collection of stories that would not only represent a range of the many talented writers who deserve to be included in an anthology such as this, but also to depict the wonderful diversity of themes and styles, the originality, and the difference from and adherence to Mexican and world-wide literary traditions.

The short story has a long tradition in Mexico. The pillars of its modern versions, Juan Rulfo, José Revueltas, and Juan José Arreola, published their works in the 1950s, the decade when many of the authors gathered in this anthology were born. In the following years, the Mexican short story was enriched by Carlos Fuentes, José Emilio Pacheco, Inés Arredondo, Edmundo Valadés, Hernán Lara Zavala, and Guillermo Samperio, among many others. Today its active participants are spread throughout the nation, and they are men and women of all ages who feel comfortable with the genre's capacity for suggestion, the dizzying effect of its structure, and the brilliance of its language. Prose workshops and short story contests serve to swell the ranks of practitioners and to increase the number of publications, including books, journals, and magazines. *Points of Departure* waters at both old and new oases, those wells of communication that have sprung up in America, where the North American short story, the Latin American "boom," and Mexico's impressive legacy have shaped sensibilites, tastes, quests.

The new Mexican short story is more urban and less tied to canonical structures. It does not reflect exotic worlds seen through the eyes of a stranger, but rather singular worlds that are even more enticing. In *Points of Departure,* one encounters a parade of ambiences and solitudes, in-group codes, diverse social strata, pleasures, and terrors, all from the perspective of modern individuals, with styles that are as diverse as the topics they treat. The love relationship and its destruction, as well as the loss of illusion and the acceptance of a more raw, crude reality are at the heart of many of these stories written by the last romantic generation of the twentieth century (a characterization I make bold to put before you), those of us who grew up between rock and roll and ingenuous dreams of utopia. The stories breathe a soft decadence, but also emanate a humor that ranges from the sarcastic to the acid-tongued. The environments are either very local or quite cosmopolitan. They are bound by landscapes of the border, the desert, and the sea, but above all by the closed-in spaces of any city: the bar, the home, the psychoanalyst's couch, a prison, a restaurant, a small business, sidewalks, and benches on the street. Perambulating through them are tropical music, rock, and silence, the mixture of the urban and the rural ever present in turn-of-the-century Mexico. Magical realism is a manifestation of the ironies of urban daily life: a cow grazes on the grass median dividing a congested boulevard, or a salesman goes to work each day with no merchandise to sell.

The writers included here come from different parts of Mexico, although the majority were born and live in Mexico City. The north is represented by noteworthy writers such as Sada, Toscana, Parra, and Conde. Five of us are women: Estrada, Conde, Krauze, Beltrán, and I, but, as the book evidences, there are still fewer female writers than male writers on the national literary scene. Many of these authors have received important literary prizes and have been translated into various languages, though most have never been published in English before. Many of them have lived or are living abroad, and their writing reflects this, as in the works by Uribe, Rivas, and Acosta. And, as always happens with anthologies, many authors who meet the criteria for inclusion (a recognized "track record," outstanding short story credentials, an original voice, actively writing) have been left out, in this case due to the effervescence of literary production throughout the nation.

Points of Departure reflects a modern, cosmpolitan world in which the personal voice of each author, each in its own cadence, speaks of the preoccupations of human beings everywhere: individuals, their solitude and their struggles are the points of departure. Diversity, vitality, and originality of expression—irreducible to some kind of simplistic exoticism as the defining element of Mexican identity—are the hallmarks of this book, where sweet hope and sordid revelation share the stage. Points of departure down the different roads the writers have taken, setting out from their most immediate heritage, obviously American in the continental sense of the word. Points of departure because the styles and the themes seem to branch out in every direction and are difficult to constrain at a homologous level.

I cannot help but feel honored in the company of the authors gathered here. My hope is that this book will repay the reader with the same pleasure that it was to produce it, stimulating his or her appetite for reading and for what is happening on the contemporary Mexican literary scene.

Mónica Lavín / Mexico City

REAL LIFE
Eduardo Antonio Parra

THIS LIFE IS DISGUSTING, SOTO SAID TO HIMSELF AS HE FLOPPED HIS BODY INTO a chair, his flesh quivering all over, feeling his weight causing his vertebrae to flatten their discs until they groaned. He lit a cigarette and noticed that his hands were no longer trembling. The sweat still exuded from his palms and between his fingers in spite of his constantly rubbing them against the nap of his jacket. In the silence of the newsroom, the image of the two cadavers again floated before his eyes. The ulcer in the pit of his stomach kicked in. Hell, let me be. He inhaled the smoke and exhaled forcefully, but he wasn't able to dispel the pain or the sight: the two inert faces in the mud, bloody and pale, their skin almost translucent in the glare of the flash. Then he saw himself coming back to the paper in the pouring rain, chain-smoking in a vain attempt to extirpate that stench of blood, sex, and alcohol that had clung to his body from the moment he entered the ruins of the movie theater.

"Soto, put out the cigarette," Ramos, the editor, said from his office.

He stomped out the butt murmuring an insult that involved the editor's mother. He looked at all the signs recently posted on all the walls: *No Smoking.* Damn, who cares about health? Orders from the new director. But who can even think of complying with rules after being at that slaughterhouse?

Two transients . . . he furiously banged the computer keys. He stopped. He deleted those words. He substituted: Two homeless persons. . . . He stopped again. Why was there no sound when he typed? Where had those heavy, noisy, metal machines gone, the ones that made you feel like you were really working? He reached for his cigarettes automatically, but he left them in his pocket as he took another look at those sanctimonious little signs.

Two transients, two homeless people, the same ones he had interviewed for a feature story some months before. Two human beings clothed in rags, who in their own way were a manifestation of the metaphor of desire: in the midst of the most abject of circumstances, they had built their own paradise, enjoyed secret pleasures, and cheated the pain. Two authentic *clochards* who lived on the street, ate out of garbage cans, slept in the parks or abandoned buildings, and fornicated wherever they pleased. A couple in the exact meaning of the term. Partners in crime against the universe. Lovers united by filth and hunger, solvents and alcohol, freedom and desire, ultimately bonded by the unadorned fact of daring to remain together.

"It's disgusting," Soto said again, out loud this time, not recognizing that hoarse voice choked with anger.

He had first seen them during a raid on a brothel disguised as a dance hall. It had been at least a year ago. Soto had gone to the place with a convoy of *judiciales*. The uniforms lined up all the fauna in the whorehouse, and he took pleasure in photographing the potheads who hid their faces, the transvestites proud of being women, the whores who offered their bodies if he could keep them out of jail. As he was jotting down the names of the detainees, the couple approached him.

"Slip us a bottle of something and we'll pose for a photo."

Their initiative pleased him, although he could not hide a gesture of revulsion: they smelled of vomit, of soaking sweat, of old shit, and from under that fetidness, another, perhaps more tender, sweeter, smell filtered out, one that Soto associated with the emanations rising from rotten fruit. Their appearance had no better effect: on both the rags barely covered their skin scattered with boils, pimples, and filthy, soft masses of black grease. She, almost bald, exhibited iridescent blemishes on her skull, very much like the wet blotches on the walls. The guy, on the other hand, displayed a full head of hair that measured a palm's length, and was tipped with something like hard, shiny shoe polish.

It seemed worth it. Soto pointed the lens at them, which stimulated the couple's exhibitionism: first they modeled for wedding pictures, she standing, her eyes filled with dreams, and he seated, his arm around her waist. Next they separated, looking lovingly into each other's eyes, holding hands. Then they crossed their arms over their shoulders, like buddies, while they smiled at the camera with tartar-covered teeth. Suddenly they kissed, and were already caressing each other under the threadbare cloth when his roll of film gave out.

Then they came up to Soto expecting him to live up to his part of the bargain, but he pretended not to notice, mumbling "some other day," because the uniformed cops were beginning to board their units.

"Answer the telephone, Soto!" Ramos screamed at him from afar.

He looked at the receiver without moving, and didn't even budge through the next few rings. I feel like smoking, not speaking to Remedios. Because it had to be Remedios. Who else would it be? Especially at this time. Wasn't it around three? This damned shift, shit. The bodies had been discovered before midnight, as someone assured him through the newspaper's scanner. Over two hours, and he still stank of death, of blood, of sex. Only the odor of alcohol had disappeared. Another ring. Yes, it had to be Remedios calling him to complain about his being late, about his bad manners in not calling to let her know. And that image of the two faces united in death wouldn't go away. Bad manners. And without being allowed to smoke. Didn't she realize he didn't want to talk to her? Sad, beaten down, in a way he hadn't been for a long time. Lack of courtesy: lack of consideration: you don't care if I can't sleep when you don't come home. I feel like getting drunk. Another ring. She can go fuck herself.

"If you don't answer it, I will," Ramos was next to him. "I'm goddamned fed up . . ."

"It's stopped ringing now."

"Haven't you written that story yet?"

3

"I'm on it, there's no rush."

The stinking story, Soto repeated under his breath as he rubbed his hands on his pants. In spite of his damp clothing and the air-conditioning that turned the newsroom into a freezer, the viscous sweat kept oozing out between his fingers and from his palms. It felt as though he had just taken them out of a can of grease. He started typing and stopped again. How was he going to write this story? How to avoid giving the impression that he had recognized the bodies? How to give it a tone of false objectivity so his readers would not realize that his own sentiments, his disgust, his disappointment were all involved? He had never developed the first photos: the roll had gotten lost in all the confusion at the media lab. And he would not have remembered them if he had not run into the couple again a few months later.

They were coming out of a little park where the bushes were tangled helter-skelter, like an empty lot. It was noon. Soto was cruising around downtown when he spotted them: arm in arm, happily caressing each other over their rags, in such a loving manner that he had no doubt about what they had been doing in the park. He felt envy: he and Remedios had long ago lost the desire to love each other that way.

He parked the car the first chance he got and followed them through the crowd for a couple of blocks, until he caught up with them in a little plaza full of beggars. There were clouds of flies buzzing everywhere. A mixture of smells — garbage, sewage, sick humanity, and putrid water — the air was thick, and assailed him right away. On the ground, the confusion of tattered blankets, the piles of very worn old clothes cast about at random, and the bodies covered with scraps of food made Soto walk as if crossing a river on stones, stepping in the clear spots, dodging the outstretched hands begging for money. At the end of this odyssey, he stood in front of the couple and asked them if they remembered him.

"Of course, fatso, you're a real heavyweight."

He got them to accompany him to a nearby liquor store and bought them two fifths of the cheapest tequila. Once back at the plaza, he offered them an interview and another photo session, but they said they would rather get peacefully drunk with their buddies. He could look them up later, since he now knew where to find them. Soto insisted. You could at least pose for a few minutes, he said. But they wouldn't pay attention to him: they had hunkered down next to some garbage cans and were generously showing the bottles to the denizens of the park as an invitation to come and drink.

"Take my picture," another vagabond grabbed him by the elbow.

He shook him off without looking at him. Now he was really fascinated with the couple: in spite of the rags and scars, in spite of all the filth in which they lived, they seemed to be able to sublimate their way to happiness. Their flesh, the desire in their bodies, sustained them in that state of grace in which they laughed, partied, shared the bottles with their friends; they hugged and kissed amidst the muck. An intense envy once again wrenched Soto's guts. Before leaving, he intercepted a man who was on his way to join the tequila party.

"Do you know those people's names?"

"No," he laughed, "but they call them the Love Birds."

The cold in the newsroom penetrated deeply, and Soto rubbed his arms. His hands began shaking again; they would not stop sweating, and now he couldn't tell if it was because of the temperature or because of his inability to fulfill his obligation to write the news story. Think, Soto, he said to himself, in an effort to concentrate, it's only one more crime in the city, just like the ones you report every day to feed the sick readers. One more aberration the people enjoy just to feel they're normal, sane, safe within the four walls of their homes. Nothing extraordinary: two vagabonds, two crazy street people, two dead John Does killed by the hand of another lowlife just like them in one of the inner-city neighborhoods. It doesn't matter that you knew them, that you had even attempted to make them famous by proclaiming to the four winds the joy and freedom in which they lived through a feature story that was hacked to pieces because nobody was interested in all that pornographic trash about two social scabs. Who cares about the good kind of envy you felt toward them, or the enthusiasm and faith in humankind they revived in you? None of it matters. It's like the sweat on your hands, the stink in your nose, the tornado in your head, and the image of the two dead bodies that you can't stop seeing. No, none of it matters, not even this desperate need to smoke, to take off running, to find a bar and wash up, to purify yourself with a bottle of rum. You've never felt anything in the face of death. Don't start now. There's no reason why; it's only a part of life. That's what you've always said.

"Did you bring graphics, Soto?" Ramos was carrying his briefcase.

"They're being developed."

"Good, when you finish the story, leave it all on Agustín's desk," he gave him a pat on the back by way of good-bye. "Tomorrow it'll be on the front page in the evening edition."

He watched him turn the corner at the end of the hallway, and listened to the echo of his footsteps for a few seconds. When silence returned to his immobility, Soto took out a cigarette and lit it. The smell of the burning tobacco curled into his nostrils, and feeling himself liberated from that other smell, the one he'd been dragging along since he left the movie house; for a moment he was able to forget the vision causing him anguish.

He had gone back to the plaza to look for them a few weeks later, very early in the morning, at an hour when the inhabitants of the esplanade had not yet abandoned their alcoholic dreams. A light fog that somewhat neutralized the fumes filled the air. It gave the scene a dismal look: men and women bunched together in a tumble of heads and rags, dirt and garbage. They looked like mummified cadavers, surprised by a rain of dust that had asphyxiated them as they slept, burning their flesh just enough to blacken them.

He snapped a few photos of the swarm. Then he began examining each one of the faces without finding the couple. He asked a fat woman, apparently the only one conscious, about them, as she lay spread-eagled on a bench, contemplating the fog. She stared at him for a long time, but said nothing. It's no use, Soto said to himself, and he looked about for a path to get away from that labyrinth of bodies, but from the ground someone grabbed him by the pant leg.

"How is she going to answer you?" the voice came out of a pile of burlap. "Can't you see she's mute?"

"And you do know where they are?"

"What ya wan'em for?"

"I have some unsettled business with them."

The burlap contracted, as though giving birth, and from within its threads a half-bald head poked out, black hair, as though painted on with rough brush strokes. It turned around and Soto saw its face: normal, except for the extremely bloodshot eyes.

"Are you going to give them a bottle for taking their picture?"

"Maybe."

"Give it to me," he said, showing off his toothless gums, "I'm way more handsome, ain't I?"

It was no use. No one was in any condition to tell him. He started walking back to his car. When he reached the street, he heard the sleepy, hoarse voice of an old woman:

"Look for them on the street back over there," she smiled roguishly, "They went to fuck. Maybe you'll catch them. You'll get hornier pictures . . ."

The ringing of the telephone made him jump and almost tumble out of his chair. Remedios again, damn it. Rubbing his hands together, he looked around to make sure he was still alone in the newsroom. The sweating persisted. Now a pain in his jaw was also plaguing him, he sleepily noticed, grinding his teeth from the tension. I get worse every day. He stood up, hearing the phone ring again. Thousands of ants crawled up his legs and began radiating heat as he walked. He went to the file room, directly to the police file. He took out a manila folder whose only label was his own surname written in pencil.

There were around sixty negatives and enough text for two full pages. When he first saw the material, Ramos had been overcome by an enthusiasm that quickly infected the designer. He praised the photos and the interview, and throwing off his usual restraint, he congratulated him for managing to recognize a sanctuary of beauty that made life bearable in the midst of all that filth. As a matter of fact, this is real life, and Ramos had immediately added, the life our readers should get to know. He assured him that on Sunday he would give it a two-page, centerfold spread, for only thus could one appreciate the magical aura that surrounded the vagabonds. The headline read "In Another Dimension" and once it was set, Ramos took it to the Chief's office.

He came back more serious than they had ever seen him: next Sunday one of the centerfold pages would announce a department store sale. What was more, they had ordered him to keep the feature story down to a maximum of half a page, because what people expected of that section was crime and accidents, not obscenity or vulgarity. What do you mean, real life? Real life was what people read in the newspaper. It would do no good to insist. The boss had decided.

Soto left the file room, folder in hand. The telephone had stopped ringing and in the newsroom the only sound to be heard were distant rumors issuing from the designers' cubicle. I have to write something for Agustín. Whatever I can. Otherwise, I could give him the information and leave him to fend for himself. Or only the graphics. As he moved toward his chair he heard the footsteps of the photo lab technician behind him.

"Hey, Soto, these are a bitch," he handed him the strips of film, "And how did that animal kill them?"

"What time is it?"

"Four."

"When does Agustín get in?

"Between four-thirty and five."

He turned his back to him and sat down. The other man stood there for a few seconds, but soon his steps sounded his retreat. In the blank space on the screen, the cursor emitted a green, intermittent, exasperating pulse. Soto left the folder on the desk and noticed that it was damp with sweat. Next to the keyboard the filmstrips curled into spirals. He did not have to check the images; he still had them tattooed on his eyeballs, ceaselessly projecting themselves onto the objects around him. Nor did he have to take the rest of them out of the folder. Those he had tattooed on his memory.

He had found them by following the old woman's instructions. It was an old, solitary street the government was going to widen to make way for an avenue. There were department stores, small shops, homes, an enormous movie house, and a couple of apartment buildings. Most were in ruins; only a few buildings still had occupants. There were lowlifes everywhere: squatting in doorways among the rubble, warming themselves around a fire, asking for money on the street corners.

Soto peered into every one of the buildings through holes that appeared to have been caused by a bombardment. He found them inside of what was once a department store, whose pulverized windows littered the floor. When he saw them, he smiled. The old woman had been telling the truth. He was resting belly-up with his tattered clothes in disorder and his breath short, as though he were suffering an attack of asthma. She, kneeling next to him, was slowly rubbing his chest, gazing tenderly upon him as she had him sip out of a bottle. If her coat had not hung all the way to the floor, Soto would have seen her naked legs.

"Oh, look, the reporter," the woman stifled a laugh with her hand. "Oh, don't tell me he's been spying on us."

The man simply widened his smile. Then he signaled Soto to come closer. The glass shards crunched under his feet, and when he reached them it surprised him that the woman was actually wearing a pair of pants that looked like moth-eaten bearskin. They offered him a rock to sit on and out of her rags she produced a plastic baggy. She breathed in and exhaled three times. Then, holding the air in her lungs, she offered it to him.

"No, I don't toke," said Soto.

"Then have a drink," the man said, giving him the bottle.

He had to conquer his repulsion and fear of that beverage. The alcohol had been cut with soda, but it nevertheless went down his throat like molten metal, a slow sensation, heavy, burning, that upon hitting his stomach liberated a wave of acid vapors. Soto coughed until he saw stars, while they, roaring with laughter, fell over backward and writhed around like children, grabbing their bellies with each gleeful spasm.

After they had calmed down, Soto pulled out his pack of cigarettes, passed it around, lit one, and turned on his tape recorder.

"First the interview," he said. "Then we take the pictures."

As they answered the questions, they toasted with a hit of weed and a drink, exchanging the baggy for the bottle. They couldn't remember how long they'd been together, partnered up, they said. The past was a kind of empty space, a blurry movie in which each in his own way played the roles of other people they had forgotten. A world of hallucination, like any nightmare. All they could remember was when they met on the street, and from then on. He protected me from two jerks who wanted to screw me, she said with her glassy-eyed look. They caught up with him, knifed him, and left him half dead; show him. The man sucked in a breath from the baggy and then uncovered his back. Soto put down the recorder and picked up his camera. There were the scars, among muck and grease spots, some of them infected. He took some pictures. That was long ago, an eternity. It was painful, of course, but it served for them to get to know each other, and from that moment on, to enjoy each other, keep each other company, protect each other. They shared everything: refuge, friends and enemies, pills, alcohol, grass when there was any, the little food they had. Yeah, sure, they were often assaulted. The gangs did it for fun, the cops for hatred, the other bums because they wanted a woman, too. It don't matter, she added, crawling all over him, I have my knight in shining armor. Every battle added more scars. Anyway, he concluded, I have so many on me one more don't count. Their voices thickened, their eyes clouded over, their movements slowed down, yet they kept on talking without any need for questions; their life was love, love, and just pure love; body, desire, company; laughing, fornicating, drugging, drinking, sometimes eating, what more could they ask for?

"Now for the pictures," Soto said when their long speeches lost the last vestiges of coherence.

Although it was difficult for them to remain standing, they happily acceded. It took some doing to repeat the poses they had struck on the day of the raid. They fell on the ground more than once, and got up slowly, choking on their laughter. Soto stopped to change the roll. In the meantime, the man finished off the booze and shattered the bottle against a rock. From that moment on they quit posing; they began kissing urgently, licking the scars on their faces, the crusts of muck. They stopped now and then to smile into the camera. Their hands came and went among the rags, caressing, squeezing.

Suddenly he put her up against the wall and covered her with his body. Quickly she pinned him with her legs, making him hump her. Soto kept working the camera, and captured the moment when their hands parted the rags to reach inside, his to her breasts, hers to his sex.

They had completely forgotten the photos and the reporter. Absorbed in themselves, they let themselves fall into the vertigo of their bodies. In spite of the hot current quickening the blood in his veins, Soto realized he was an intruder, alien to that world constituted by only two beings. He took a few more pictures before he noticed they had dropped their tattered clothing on the ground. For a second he felt sorry for those two skeletons dressed in their beaten-up skin, saturated with old and new scars, blotched with infections. But as he saw the desire with which they groped each other, his sentiment succumbed to the uneasiness churning in his guts. Perturbed by a growing excitement, he was shamed into running away from that place.

He went back to the liquor store for two more bottles of tequila. It was the right thing to do. To calm his anxiety, he filled his lungs with the fresh, humid air of the street. A little calmer, he returned to the old store, where the heavy breathing awakened an adolescent innocence in him. He tried not to make noise as he stepped on the glass, and without turning toward the couple, he left the bottles in a visible spot. He did not see them, but he did smell them; the stench of rotten fruit that he had perceived on the two of them before was now more intense than ever. No wonder, he said to himself, smiling happily. In parting, he took that fragrance with him, as well as the long, strident cry of the woman and the guttural sounds of the man.

He rubbed his eyes in a gesture of defeat. Agustín would show up soon, and the screen was still blank. A cigarette shook between his fingers, and his eyes followed the smoke until it reached the ventilator in the ceiling. Nevertheless, what he was actually seeing was the ruins of that movie house situated on the same street where he had done the interviews. The two bodies naked, like the last time he saw them, but now soaked in blood, sunk in the mud from the force of the blows that ended up disfiguring them. The whole scene multiplied in the filmstrip spiral next to the screen. Damn, they didn't deserve it. The ashes were gaining on the tobacco in his cigarette. He flicked them on the floor and took a puff. His ulcer burned more and more. They hadn't owed anybody anything. They were free, happy. He closed his eyes and saw the dead bodies again, surrounded by reporters, cops, paramedics, and gawkers. No bums, not one of their buddies from the park. They're probably scared, Soto said to himself. The camera flashed its lightning bolts, one after another, electrifying the raindrops falling through the holes in the roof. His camera was intent upon recording every blow, the broken bones, and the swollen flesh. Why so much rancor, so much brutality? Who could hate them so? To one side, away from the circle of lights and onlookers, the murderer lay in the mud, with his hands handcuffed behind him. He had wounds on his face and wore only a pair of unbuttoned pants. They caught him raping the dead man, one of Soto's colleagues informed him, and he had already raped the woman's dead body. Damned maniac. That was why the *judiciales* punched him out.

The cigarette had burned away between his fingers. He threw the filter into a corner and searched his pockets for another. Nothing. Sick son of his whore mother. He crumpled the pack and threw it in the same direction. What had they done to you? Was it from pure envy? The faces that had laughed before were now motionless, monstrous. Hell, why so much rage? he repeated as he mulled over the arguments with which the murderer responded to the federal policeman's questions: Why did you kill them? Who knows? What do you mean who knows, punk? Well, it's just that . . . Didn't you have any motive? They were assholes; they wouldn't give me a drink. Then you did it to steal their bottle? Yeah, that's why. Then why'd you fuck them? I'd wanted to for a long . . . Both of them? Are you a fag or something? No, only the chick. And him? Why'd you fuck him too, you stinking degenerate. Just so's not to let him go to waste; he was already down, real quiet; you don't get a chance at some of that every day . . .

Soto felt nauseated. He stood up and took a few steps around the newsroom. The murderer was another bum from the esplanade. According to the police, he was extremely intoxicated. Sniffing paint thinner, on dope, pills, and who knows what else. But, hell, you just can't justify it. He sat down again, running his fingers through his hair. He could not describe any of that; he just couldn't. His eyes shot with disdain, the cynical expression with which he stared at the people standing around him became more pronounced when he saw the reporter come toward him. He gathered himself up and his mouth broke into a vile, toothless grin. You gonna take my picture now? he jeered when he saw the camera. You won't say no this time? Now I look handsome to you, don't I? He recognized him just as one of the feds gave him a hard whack, slamming him into the mud, and then the words he said were no longer those of a demented creature, but those of this pretender accusing him of complicity. The guilt was like a stab in his stomach. He lowered the camera as he felt his blood thicken in his veins. With muddled steps, he looked for the exit from the movie house. Still lying on the ground, the crazy bum watched Soto leaving and said to him, "Hey, you owe me that bottle . . ."

On the screen appeared, in detail, the same swollen, bloodshot eyes, the mouth with its naked gums, the head brushed with black paint. He turned off the computer and gave a start as he heard steps sounding in the silence. There's Agustín and I haven't done a thing. He suddenly thought he heard a countdown. Why do I get so upset? From the other side of the newsroom a figure appeared, but it wasn't Agustín; the watchman was doing his rounds.

"You still here?"

"Yeah, I got the graveyard shift. What time is it?"

"Just about five."

Minutes to go. Agustín would want to see the graphics and read the story right away. He'd been ordered by Ramos to send what Soto would leave him as the lead story. But it wasn't fair that they should see them that way, naked, violated. He picked up the filmstrip and held it up to the light: images of the kind the chief and the readers liked. "Bloody Crime of Passion," would be the headline, and Agustín would send the bloodiest, the most macabre photo to fill up the half page. No, they don't deserve it. I am not going to let it happen. Determined, he took his lighter out of his bag and set the filmstrips on fire.

The film burned rapidly, filling the air with a greasy, heavy odor. He let it fall into the trash basket and smiled as he watched the last traces of the crime being consumed. At almost the same moment, he felt his physical problems abate. The pains in his ulcer and his jaw vanished, his muscles relaxed with voluptuous relief. The bodies, the blood, the stench of death, and the cynical face of the mad murderer lay in the bottom of the trash can, turned to ashes.

Real life . . . He remembered the chief's words. Then he opened the manila folder and took out the old pictures. Let someone else break the news of the crime, the bodies, the murderer. He chose the best; the ones in which the couple brimmed with tenderness, hugged, smiled, showed off their immense happiness before the world. He clipped them to the text of his feature story and left them on Agustín's desk. They'll fire me tomorrow, for sure. He rubbed his hands together and noticed they were dry, no sweat. He smiled again. He was walking toward the exit, relieved, clear-headed, when the phone rang. Remedios again. Or Ramos. Or Agustín. Or news of another crime. Or an accident. . . . They can all go to hell.

QUEEN OF SHADOWS
Bernardo Ruíz

to L and L

WE WOMEN WHO GET CONVICTED DO OUR TIME IN TEPEPAN PRISON. THERE are more than two hundred of us in here. The trial, the hope of hearing the words, "Not guilty. You're free to go," has all been left behind. After a brief initiation, we find ourselves entering the labyrinth of a different kind of time, a very long time, much longer than time on the outside, a time in which only our thoughts and the images of our lives survive. And, although I say "we," each of us is alone, very much alone, even those who fall in love and pair off.

Passing through a series of bars, gates, and access codes, you arrive at depression, the intense desire to die, because this just can't be true. Luck can't be this cold-eyed beast reminding you day after day: "You're here; you'll never escape my jaws." And you can't even figure out how to die; you're so sad, it's as if you were anesthetized.

I used to talk to Angel Miguel, to Angel Miguel's spirit, and I would ask him why it was that he could be good and peaceful in his grave, why was it that the soldiers had managed to shoot him, what pact had he made with the bullets? Then I would hate him because he'd left me all alone, because he'd betrayed me, because I was left holding the whole bag of trouble, isolated, forgotten by the other traffickers, with the bitterness of his absence. All the punishment came down on me, the beatings and the manhandling by the judicial

15

police, getting raped by the *comandante,* and all the other violations, and then, as a tip for services rendered, they warned me I'd better not say anything to the Human Rights Commission. I was numbed against any pain life could inflict, because without Angel Miguel I'd been left with nothing.

Unable to feel, I didn't give a damn about anything. If at times I cried, it was because I'd been left alone, with my dream of a life like we all dream about: happy, without worries or cares. And what I got was to bear all the presumed and supposed guilt—possession of weapons restricted to military use, resisting arrest, aggravated assault, transporting illegal drugs, and homicide—guilt which one day became charges at the judge's discretion, and finally turned into a sentence. Thirty years in prison. An enormous sentence.

To console me, the other girls would say, "Don't worry, you get time off for good behavior; they'll reduce your sentence." And Merle said, "Give me a hand. Take this little ribbon, tie a bow, like this, a small one. Good. Now this one, again, the same way. Good." So we tied bows, lots of bows. Sometimes gazing at the top of the wall with a blank stare, trying to catch a glimpse of the horizon. Other times my eyes brimmed with tears because life was outside and I was in here, making bows with Merle, for cigarettes, for a shampoo that wouldn't ruin my hair, for some face cream. And I kept right on feeling sad.

I didn't care about those silly bows. Merle did, because it was the only thing she knew how to do. She got a kick out of tying them, as she invented stories, thinking out loud:

"This one will go on a teeny pink bikini, an almost invisible *tanguita.* The girl who wears it will have an affair, her first romance, with a singer from the coast, who'll whisper in her ear, 'I'm going to unleash your passion.' And she'll let herself be touched. She'll help him strip her, and with her singer she'll romp all over a big white bed, happy, bathed in sunshine. She'll never forget my little bow."

She would tell a thousand stories like that, one for each bow she tied, as though each ribbon had to have its own inescapable, secret spell cast upon it.

But Merle never talked about herself, never told her own story. Why was she here with me and the others?

One morning, while we were cleaning the dorm area, Xochitl told Merle's story. She had suffered her husband's blows and drunken binges for years. A man who drank himself out of his mind every day. Sometimes he didn't come home, which was okay, because when he did, if he was very drunk, he'd get an irresistible letch for one of his daughters. Merle would have to defend them, lock them up, keep them away from him and take the beatings, the animal's kicks, and pacify him any way she could.

One time he threatened her with a knife and managed to tie her up, and then it was easy to terrify and rape the girls. Later, he passed out cold from all the alcohol.

The girls untied their mother and helped her to hang their father. Merle planned the girls' escape and her own silence. She cut up the body, stuffed it into garbage bags, cruised empty fields for three nights and emptied the remains into culverts. She cleaned her house and filled other bags with his clothing, which she donated to the church clinic.

She didn't wear mourning clothes; she was careful to keep up the appearance of having been abandoned. She got a job with a friend of one of her daughters' godmothers, preparing meals in a popular eatery. She was just beginning to forget the bad days when she was investigated. Her husband's mistress had reported the man's disappearance. The dates matched, there was the unexplained absence from the factory where he worked, the neighbors' statements, everything pointing to Merle, although there was no corpus delecti. When she confessed to the deed, she denied that her daughters had been present. They managed to find a couple of the bags as proof of her statements.

I felt a lot closer to Merle after listening to Xochitl. And as I looked at her, it even seemed that the little bows she tied with such patience were of unsurpassed excellence.

"Do you believe all that about not knowing what you have until you lose it, Merle?"

"Only when it comes to things. What I miss are things. An armoire my mother had. A beautiful mirror my father gave me for my fifteenth birthday . . ."

"I miss people. I miss my mother. I miss Angel Miguel."

"It doesn't do any good to miss people. There'd be too many ghosts traipsing around these corridors. Look at this bow—it's for a movie actress's brassiere. Everybody'll see it; they'll admire her. Her movie will be a great success. She appears just like that, almost nude, to meet an engineer who steals her away, heart and all."

With so many stories, why not dream a bit? Why content yourself with what's on your rap sheet, with the few pleasant memories of your life, scenes or moments that wear out with the passage of time? You get scared to touch them, to say anything about them, for fear of their turning to dust, of someone stealing them, of having some other woman claim them as her own.

It'll drive you crazy. Better, really, to invent other tales and poke around in someone else's stories. Sometimes I read or write letters for the women who don't know how. They're grateful and think I'm a very good person. They don't realize that I'm just doing it to have someone to call "dearest," to whom to say "I miss you." Just so I won't forget that sweet words still exist.

Angel Miguel had begun to let me down, seldom appearing except in an occasional nightmare, which always ended with my burying him again. Like I had in all the others. Sometimes I buried him in the city, other times in the mountains.

He finally stopped coming back when I dug his grave in the desert, near Real de Catorce. He rested in peace, and I was left with my empty despair and longing.

Xochitl told me I needed a man. Only a man can cure the sensation of gray, rainy days that flood one's thoughts with torrents of water, with currents under the skin that drag one toward death. But I had no one to send a letter to.

Three times a day, on my way to the dining hall, I would pass by the blue and red mailboxes. I saw them there, next to the telephones, like two colored garbage cans they would take outside and empty every day.

"Find yourself someone," Xochitl advised.

She, of course, had her husband in the Reclusorio Norte, the facility on the city's north side. And Thursday was visiting day. And with good behavior they could even have Tuesdays, Saturdays, or Sundays. Holidays.

"It's not so bad being your man's accomplice," Xochitl commented, "at least when they nail you, you know they'll be watching him for you."

"Sure, if they don't blow him away first," I protested. The visions of the mountains came back to me, and the ambush, that moment that can't be put into words because it's all noise, fear, bullets, windows shattered into shrapnel, the lukewarm sensation of pissing on myself, the rocks, the cries of pain; I'm shooting and being shot at, and Angel Miguel is bleeding, part of his brain soiling my blouse. I burst into tears, and a profound chill creeps up my legs. All of this in just an instant.

One day Merle got sick. They took her over to the dispensary. And the doctor said she was dying, that she had cancer of the liver, that it was incurable. Call my daughters, she said.

I dialed her neighbor's number.

"This is Anastasia, Señora Merle's cellmate; she's sick and she's asking me to inform her daughters. . . . Yes, very sick."

And I realized that I still had a name. I learned that I was alive. Someone could find me.

I am Anastasia. I was a dancer. I am twenty-eight years old (you always have to subtract a few years), *and I am locked up in Tepepan Women's Prison. I am alone and without friends. I would like to meet you. Will you visit me this Thursday?*

I clung to that hope. Someone in this world could become interested in me, the way Angel Miguel had. Like a madwoman, any time I had a free moment and some money, I would run to the telephone, dial a random number, and if a man answered, I would begin, "I am Anastasia . . ."

They often hung up. I heard curses and insults. They made fun of me. They told me off. I kept on. A new number.

I am Anastasia. I was a dancer. I am twenty-eight years old and I am locked up in Tepepan Women's Prison. I am alone. Would you visit me some day?

Five, six, even eight attempts daily. Whispering, so the other women in line wouldn't hear me. Claiming the phone was busy; give me a break. Some days I was sure I had a seductive voice, irresistible. Other days I was sad, almost certain I was only going to hear negative comments and contempt. And Xochitl would say, "Find a man." And the absence of Merle, who died at midnight. I am Anastasia.

Xochitl was sleeping. Delfina, who is not my friend, was awake, and she propped herself up on her elbows when the matron came by to tell us. Merle's empty bed and an almost complete silence that was probably coming from me. But I felt Merle walking down the aisle and I called to her in a low voice, to bid her farewell.

"Say hello to my mother. Say hello to Angel Miguel, if you see them."

And Merle smiled at me and asked me to tell her a story. Something new she could tell on the other side. I had only my own at hand, Anastasia's tale.

So then I told her about the girl from a convent school who, fifteen years ago at the age of sixteen, ran away from the city of Culiacan to Tijuana for the love of Angel Miguel. And since Anastasia danced with style and grace, she was able to support her companion while they organized a crew to smuggle grass over to the other side of the border.

The exhausting days of work at the outset went by relatively quickly. In a few months the couple had a beautiful apartment, like the ones you see on television. And things got even better when they got into the pill business. Anastasia got pregnant at nineteen, but lost the child. She got so depressed that she decided never to have any more babies so she wouldn't have to cry over them.

They were tipped off that they were going to be busted. They ran off to Guadalajara. That was the most peaceful time of her life. Angel Miguel was a talented man, and he went about widening his contacts. He was respected and he seldom had to put his merchandise at risk. In order to get into the business on a grand scale, he took on Panamanian partners.

We had money to burn. We bought a lot of things, an ice factory in Colima, a restaurant in Queretaro, two airplanes, an apartment in Mexico City, the supermarkets in Campeche, and a farm in Chiapas. The Central Americans were good partners and had managed to avoid the latest attempts at controlling the trade. The demand and the risks kept growing. We had to watch the shipments closely. You couldn't leave anything to luck, much less trust anyone who wasn't connected. I threw myself wholeheartedly into the business.

Now, that's where you're learning something every day. You're constantly inventing new tricks. The adventure is thrilling, as though you were going 200 mph in the midst of a storm. A frenzy you can't postpone. You're alive. You're an arsenal and a target. You're feared and fearful. You know that any moment could be your last. And you know you're eternal, impassioned, a winner every time you get laid or make love.

That's life, until they catch someone. And he sings. He tells all. And you just barely escape with the evidence. There's a lot of money at stake, and you're the one carrying it.

Your pursuers will chase you until they have you surrounded on a mountain pass and they'll shoot at you. And you'll lose it all, Anastasia: your man, your youth, your money. That's the story of Anastasia.

"There's a bow on the corner of my blanket. I made it for you."

Merle left slowly, as though life were still hurting her. Xochitl, Queta, and Delfina were still asleep. I took the little bow and hid it between my breasts.

My luck did not change soon. I went back to the telephone. I tried again.

I am Anastasia. I was a dancer. I am twenty-eight years old and I am locked up in Tepepan Women's Prison. I am alone. I would like to meet you. Would you visit me Thursday?

There were days when dialing was just a reflex. I stuck to the first sentence like an addict to his fix: I am Anastasia. Anastasia was beginning to feel that she wasn't Anastasia any more. But I had to look for my man. The last one had been under the earth for an endless time. I hardly knew his name anymore.

I keep the notebook with the numbers. The telephone numbers I tried before I got to yours. A thick notebook, with big numbers, all crossed out except for the last one. Your phone number: 555-1754. A telephone in the northern part of the city. At the other end of the city from where my bedroom is, and my bed.

"I am Anastasia. I was a dancer. I am twenty-eight years old and I am locked up in Tepepan Women's Prison. I am alone, desperate, and without friends. I would like to meet you. Would you visit me on Thursday?"

21

"Sure, with pleasure," said the deep, calm voice.

I froze, paralyzed, beside myself. I was barely able to go on. I got scared. Like when a helicopter is chasing you out in the open fields and you have nowhere to hide. I shook like a girl who has wanted to become a woman for years, and when she discovers that she finally is one, she thinks she's dying. If Anchondo hadn't poked me from behind, my three minutes would have been up.

"You really would come? Don't tease me. I'm asking you for real."

"Really, I promise. My name is Iordi, Iordi Ezaguirre. Is that the name you use, Anastasia? Should I ask for you?"

"Anastasia Cervera, Iordi."

"Do you want me to bring you anything?"

It was a dream. I felt like falling flat on my back. I never thought I would get to ask for anything.

"I don't know, a fashion magazine, shampoo, some chocolate candy."

"I'll look you up on Thursday, then, about eleven, Anastasia."

"Please. Don't let me down."

I walked around out of it all day Monday. I didn't even eat, or anything. All I did was go over my conversation with Iordi, over and over again. I dared inform the administration that I would have a visitor on Thursday. I think I was happy, very happy. I felt a foolish happiness that I had no reason to feel. But only a gentleman offers a gift without asking anything in return.

That night at lights out, the fear returned. This time it was an atrocious fear. The fear of disappointment. Because if he broke his promise, I would hate him. I would hate myself. Even if he had an excuse for not coming, I would never forgive him. I felt like a jerk, hateful. I wished that Thursday would never come, that Tuesday's sun would never rise.

And then, what? Yes, then what? They come and go. I've seen it with other women. They bathe, they primp, they ask you to give them a manicure, or to cut and style their hair. You see them there, nervous. They wait all day long. Nothing. No visitor. They go back to their room and pick a fight. They get punished. They seem to come out of it. But their frustration and anger are obvious in their odor, in their sexual heat, in their every gesture. And they wait again in anxious anticipation. But now without hope.

I felt for my notebook under my pillow. What if he's a sonofabitch and we don't understand each other? What if he's an old pig? What if I don't like him? What's this all about?

I didn't sleep. I counted Xochitl's snores, Delfina's asthmatic breaths. I counted the warm sighs of the new girl, Queta. I recalled Merle's bows. I tried to remember which bow she had given me, which spell. In the dark I couldn't tell if I was wearing one of my own bows, one with no charm at all, or the one I inherited from Merle. Amidst such fantasies and anguish, Thursday arrived. And with Thursday came the appointed hour, and with the hour, Iordi.

When I saw him, I froze. My body heat escaped to the sky. A soft shudder ran through me, as though they had just put out all the lights in the world and a spotlight followed every step I took toward a body wrapped in shadows at center stage before a packed house. Countless pairs of eyes around me, their gaze fixed upon me, and the rhythmic sound of my steps resounding on the wood in the midst of a total silence you could cut with a knife.

He knew it was me, and he wanted me to know that it was him looking right at me, only moving his lips, saying soundlessly, "Anastasia?"

And Anastasia was once again the *bailaora*, the gypsy, the white crane cutting across the sky, the incarnation of the *cante jondo*, the dark-eyed lioness capable of defeating the night, the desert, and death itself. I had fixed myself up for him. So young, almost a boy. And he was so beautiful to me, I wanted him for my own. Forever.

"I am Anastasia," I said to him, taking his arm, taking him for a walk with me, "This is where I spend my days, where I work, sleep, eat, and dream. A long time ago I killed the men who ambushed my husband. He died. I'm alone."

Iordi smiled, as though he understood the whole story, as though he thought I'd done right. I heard his voice, low, deep, slow, describing landscapes full of light and shadows, an immense house full of marble and chandeliers, wide windows, cold, all too tidy since the death of his father, a great painter whom he had admired, who had lived on in his memory for the last ten years.

Surrounded by gardens and canyons, the house was situated in a corner of the world. His mother took care of it. She was a strange, cold woman who shunned social life and contact with people.

"And what do you do there? I can only imagine you walking, sleeping, eating supper, or climbing stairs. You speak to me of a place. What do you do? How do you live?"

He had always lived in that house. With his older brother and his sister, both of whom were married now. She lives in the United States. He in Mexico. But they rarely see each other. Iordi studies industrial design, likes to daydream, hardly sees anyone, and draws on his computer. He talks about his computer a lot. I interrupt him and ask him about his girlfriends. He blushes and tells me he doesn't have any. Crazy me, I tell him I believe him. We are silent for a while. Full of questions and doubts.

"Will you visit me again?"

He says yes and smiles. I explain something he really doesn't know about, so he'll know what to say to the warden. He should know that at first he should visit me as a friend. And I feel myself blushing. His gaze sparkles and he blushes too. He looks down. We end up laughing. Nerves. Happiness. I say to him, "It's so good you said yes."

I kiss him, quickly, lightly, only to feel his lips and learn his smell. He says good-bye with a hug. I hear his trembling voice in my ear, "Anastasia, do you know you're very attractive?"

He leaves. His visit is over. I feel like a lake after springtime has returned.

I press the bow I will let him see some morning against my body. I go back to my room.

At first, Iordi comes only on Thursdays. His presence will become more frequent. His gifts are surprises, perfumes or toys he designs for me, earrings or fantastic engravings, books with photographs of imaginary places. My wonder grows with each visit. He shows me astonishing worlds, and explains everything that goes through his mind. "Don't you talk to anyone?" I ask. "Only to you, Anastasia."

Anastasia teaches Iordi about love. She helps him discover fascination. The bewitchment of desire. Thursdays and weekends become days of madness. A freedom unknown to her and to him springs from the intertwining of their bodies. Anastasia blooms magnificently in the shelter of her man.

He silently hates his society, "It's like a movie. Everyone has his role and always stays in character. Their manners are a way of showing they're empty, prisoners in some delusion or another," he confesses with rancor, in a voice full of bitterness. "I prefer loneliness. Let them think I'm conforming. Some day I'll disappear."

At times Anastasia doesn't know what he's talking about. And at others she remembers when she left Culiacan under the cover of night, in the safety of Angel Miguel's arms. She tells him it's all right. That at twenty-two, or at sixteen, one does what one has to do.

As the months have gone by, Iordi has changed. Now he blushes at his blushing so easily before. And I discover in him a secret, unshakeable confidence behind his timid gestures.

With him I have learned to laugh again, and to draw, and I'll do it well to fill my wall with images of Iordi and my notebook with the beautiful letters of his name. I am happy. Marillac, one of the other girls, lends me her books of poems and I copy the most amorous ones to mail to him, as a surprise, and so he'll remember me, and so he won't forget me.

The girls call me pretentious or crazy, jokingly, and I answer that that's what happens when you follow Xochitl's advice. I know they envy me without ill will. I offer them my candy and chocolates, and I promise them they'll all be my bridesmaids when we get married.

One Thursday comes and goes without Iordi and I go insane. I dial 555-1754 and no one answers. I feel threatened. I write one, two, three letters. Despair, impotence, and sleeplessness invade me. And I call on Friday and no one answers.

The weekend is dreadful. A recording tells me the telephone has been disconnected, to call another number for information. Calmly, another voice tells me that information can't give me any information about that number or the new number. I curse its mother.

Iordi doesn't come back the next week, and I'm left without news. Even my friends avoid me. I know Xochitl won't tell me to find a man anymore. And if any one of them dares suggest that I find myself a woman, I'll scratch her eyes out.

I cry. I don't understand. And the less I understand, the more I cry. And to top it all off, they tell me the warden wants to see me. I go begrudgingly. On her desk are my letters.

She doesn't even ask me to sit down.

"Your visitor's mother came by. She wanted to know where he is," pointing to my letters, "and she wants me to stop him from coming here because, according to her, the boy and you are not equals. I can't prohibit that. Is that clear?"

I nod. The warden is younger than me. I keep quiet. I'm waiting. She hasn't signaled for me to leave.

"The lady wants to talk to you."

"Tell the stinking old lady that we are not equals."

She gives me permission to go. I go to my room. I cry, I cry alone. My soul is a disjointed mannequin crawling around in the shadows. I let sadness envelope me; it possesses me like a dense, eternal fog.

Three weeks without news. Until this afternoon, when they handed me an envelope. It had a gringo stamp on it. In the envelope, a photograph a little bigger than a postcard. It's the image of a gypsy Virgin Mother, crowned, in mourning, dressed in black clothes. Behind her, a light. On the other side, his handwriting. Over his name, two lines:

"My most beloved, my longed-for Anastasia:
My Queen, I will come back for you on Thursday, the 11th.
                                                          Iordi

It is now midnight of the 10th. The waiting is not over yet. There are still a few hours left. I squeeze the tiny bow my Merle left me. "The owner of this bow shall be called the Queen of Shadows, and she shall find her king. He shall be the light for her. They shall find each other by chance, and love shall be theirs.

26

He shall learn manliness from her, and for her he shall be able to burn down the most splendid palace and conquer any foe. In order for them to be together, beyond chance, he must walk uncertain paths. If he survives the ambushes, he shall have run the wide circle that takes him to the Queen's castle. He shall walk through the portals. Trembling, he shall untie this bow in order to view the intimate beauty of the woman who shall be, forever, his wife."

I'm waiting, Iordi, I'm waiting.

JUNE GAVE HIM THE VOICE
Josefina Estrada

MEDARDO APPROACHED HIS WIFE'S STILL-WARM CORPSE. HE PRIED AN ENVE-lope from her fingers that said: *To be opened after my death.* He took off her glasses. He picked up the book of poems. He sat in front of the woman and by way of a prayer, stammered: *"June, you who did not bear your promised fruit of sacrifice . . ."* His hands, unable to hold the book, let it fall.

He got up to prepare a cup of coffee. He took the envelope out of his pocket and, without opening it, he set fire to it and used it to light the pilot light on the stove; he dropped it into the sink, where it continued to burn. While the water boiled, he cleaned up the ashes, repeating those words inces-santly. He returned to the study. His coffee got cold. *"June gave me the voice, the silent music to quiet a sentiment."*

Raquel won't take her eyes off me. Her teeth tear off bits of a pear that roll down her sweater and fall into her lap, where she picks them up and chews them some more. The juice dilutes yesterday's chocolate. There's blood on the pulp of the fruit; it hurts her gums, but she goes on eating desperately; she spits the chewed-up skin into her hand and puts it into her mouth again. How does she manage to chew so noisily with the five teeth she has left? If she would only stop moving her head from side to side. She looks at me with sur-prise, and without stopping her eating, says to me:

"Get off. It's mine, you understand? Mine."

"What did you say? What's yours?"

"The chair. Get up. It belongs to me."

I get up. Last week she got into her head that the food belonged to her, and she wouldn't let me eat. I decided to feed myself while she sleeps. I wish she would decide that the bed was hers so I could avoid . . . well, she is my wife and hasn't always been this way. She was never interested in finery. Vanity didn't affect her; she only spent the obligatory time looking in the mirror. Now she spends hours staring at her reflection with her face up against the foggy mirror. She pretends not to know the hazy face, turns her back to it, but when she looks again she always finds it there. Bothered, almost indignant, she tries to improve her features tracing them with her index finger. When the mirror dries, grotesque signs appear, frightening her, and crying, she licks her reflection. The flies land on the glass. She tries to trap them, but she's so blind . . .

"Put on your glasses. That way you can kill them."

"Who's talking to you? How do you know I want to tear them apart? Oh! You're spying on me! Now you spy on me. First you try to starve me to death and then you spend your time watching me. Look, it's best you know: I won't torture them. Besides, I don't need glasses. You think I'm blind?"

And she leaves, tripping over the furniture, followed by the flies. I don't know how to tell her that she should bathe; it would calm her nerves. Besides, that smell of urine doesn't help her at all. It's too much for her, she just can't make it to the toilet anymore: standing, sitting, wherever she is, she just does it. At first she would get embarrassed and even tried to clean it up. Now she enjoys it: she squints and breathes a sigh of relief when she finishes. Sometimes she pulls up her skirt—she doesn't use underwear—and squats to watch the urine leak out. Then she sits next to the puddle and washes her hands and feet in it. What's she doing now? It looks like she's asleep. Yes, as always, after eating, and that pear . . . it looked good; I bought it for myself. She's never liked them, but the minute she saw it, she went for it, and I knew better than to even think of saying, "It's mine." I don't want her scratching me again. Last Monday, during breakfast, she jumped me when I reached for my roll. I was just about to take a bite when she started yelling:

"Thief, crook, rip-off artist! How dare you gobble up what doesn't belong to you! How can you steal an old woman's bread!"

All the while she was beating on me; she threw her coffee at me and scratched my face. She almost knocked me off my chair. I tried to calm her down, but her look scared me. I don't really know if she recognized me or not, if at that moment I looked like a stranger to her and because of that, she attacked me. At least that day she didn't know who I was, because other times she would say:

"Medardo! Leave that alone. The tortillas are for me, and the milk, the ham, everything you see there. And don't expect even . . . pay attention: not even the leftovers, because not even . . ."

Well, I should understand that it's her nerves, that she's sick; if not, how do you explain her saying: "You're not even as good as a dog." It's better that I eat while she's sleeping so we avoid the squabbles. How I'd like to slurp up some hot soup! Or a tasty stew. It's been years since I put something good in my stomach. . . . When she suffered her first heart attack—how long ago was that—five, seven years, or something like that—she quit cooking. I asked her to teach me. She got offended. "I'm no good to you as a woman . . . not for the other thing, not for cooking. I'm just a burden." I thought she would recuperate faster if she would rest. I made sure that she only moved when she had to, that she stayed in bed and didn't get up for anything. Then she got better and the doctor said she could live a normal life, if she didn't push herself too hard, of course. I think cooking once a week isn't too much work, that's what I believe and that's why I suggested it to her, but she put me off with her, ""I'm no good to you as a woman any more." And it went on from there. She stopped going to the market, cleaning the furniture, tidying herself up. The good thing was that by then I had retired and so I felt less of a load. At first I was more motivated to keep the house tidy.

This cheese tastes awful! I think it's rancid, but oh well, it's the only thing in the pantry. Tomorrow I'll buy the best cheese and maybe even a little wine. . . . Yes, it was good to keep the house clean because children used to come over for literature and grammar lessons. Back then, times weren't quite as bad. Then the students became fewer. I took the sign out of the window . . . nobody's interested in literature any more. Oh, but if it weren't for literature . . . It sounds like she's awake. I'd best go to my study. It's the only place where she still hasn't dared harass me, yet. She's almost deaf, but she might overhear.

Here, among my books, the world seems more deaf and blind to me. Only they know, speak, and see. My eyes and words were only good for making me a literature teacher; to teach what others wrote. Oh, Medardo, Medardo, my boy, you're going to start on your litany of frustrations! It's a fact, there's no doubt that you never wrote even a little book, not even a common manual of grammar and spelling. . . . Well, not a common one, a well-written one that would be a required textbook. A special one for every teaching level: elementary, middle, high school, and college. Thus, everyone who set foot in a school would have studied the famous *Manual of Professor Medardo Martínez Mercado.* That single title would have yielded you enough royalties to live quietly after fifty, dedicated to writing poems.

Oh, my boy, time has flown and still you haven't been able to finish your collection of poems! Oh go on, don't be so vain, not even a single poem. Medardo, be modest. Okay, okay, I'll be honest, not even a single verse. Pellicer said it: *"What is an adjective for, if all things can be seen clearly from their four sides."* And, as I say: what the poet says, let no mortal gainsay.

I don't know what it is about *Hours of June,* I don't like all the poems, but there are some, what the heck! The good poet can afford the luxury of writing what he wants how he wants. This poem, how many times did I read it to Raquel! When we were newlyweds, back then in '37, when the volume was just published:

> *Thank you,*
> *because upon my lips of thirty years*
> *you have placed pleasure and silence.*

Or this other one:

> *The anguish of being alone one lone day*
> *Opens my eyes for me at night.*

And this one, too . . . oh! the *Hours of June*. The month of my wedding and my birth: long afternoons, rainy sunshine. Red sunsets, cold mornings. What a month June is! My life has passed me by while waiting for Junes. But to tell the truth, eighty-two seem more than enough. Who's that in there? Raquel, is that you, Raquel? Answer me, woman. I forget she's deaf. Eh? What's that? Let me see. Yes, it's a mouse. I'll handle it before I go to bed; I don't want to be distracted now, I ought to write, finish the poem; without meter, without artifice. Well, not precisely a poem. Some well-written lines at least, something that when it's published would not prompt people to say, "No wonder his students left him."

It was her fault. There were times she wouldn't let them in. Especially the women; she would yell at them, "Streetwalkers, whores, fancy women, night flowers . . ." And other things that would scandalize even the most vulgar people. I never knew that my wife knew so many and such bad words. And that time she waited on the balcony for a female student to arrive, one who especially bothered her. Wasn't she about to pour a pot of boiling water on her? Right there, yes, and she didn't stop there. There was the day she got it into her head to show up naked in the middle of class. That day the students weren't women, but three young boys. I didn't even have time to cover her up and get her out of there, I was so shocked. She crossed the parlor, and as she passed between us she stopped, turning around very slowly with her hand on her hip; as she turned to leave, she said something like, "You think you're the only one who can play this game?"

I have never wanted to be young as much as I did that afternoon. I wished I were strong enough to slam straight those bodies bent over with laughter, celebrating the free show that Raquel had given them. My amazement stopped me from throwing them out or even babbling some excuse. They decided to leave. I remember trying to stop them before they reached the door, not to continue the lesson, but to speak to them about my wife's young body. Calling out their names, I asked them to come back:

"No, Prof, the class is over. We learned that 'old woman' is written with a W as in 'wrinkled wreck.'"

"What, oh, you mean . . . ?"

"Better be seeing you. Say good-bye to the old raisin."

They left, and I could still hear them out on the street:

"Oh, yeah, my little raisin, make me rise."

"I'm risin', raisin."

"Oh my, what have you there? That raisin's risin' all right!"

"She's been raised so many times she's past raisin'."

From my window I watched them making fun, fooling around. I wasn't furious anymore. I wanted to catch up with them, walk with them and leave behind the teacher and his wife. When night came, my hands were still clamped to the windowsill. My stubborn brain kept bringing me memories of Raquel's figure when she was young, foolishly recalling my tongue making proud nipples rise, retracing her contours, hoping to find some forgotten memory in her corners. . . . And so many things that, far from eliciting pleasure, only make one sad. But not even on that occasion was I able to reconstruct her features. I know she was pretty, that when she smiled her lips, being so thin, disappeared. I've forgotten her face. There are no photographs. I've spent many nights awake, blaming myself for forgetting her features and feeling ashamed that her body is so clear in my mind.

She has forgotten time; that's why she still kisses me at night. Her cracked lips rest on mine and I hold my breath so as not to smell her. Her hands rub my body. She gets on top of me; she probes me from top to bottom. Her bones dig into my belly. I don't stop her: she feels my frigidity and she soon tires, although she goes right on squashing me. And I hate myself. Because in that state she reminds me of a vulture on its carrion.

You got up before dawn, taking care not to wake him. You went to the studio, as you had been doing for some time. Through the keyhole you would watch him writing, reading, speaking. Quietly, you rummaged around in the trash can and found various pieces of wastepaper. Even with your glasses on, you couldn't figure out a thing. The persistence with which Medardo was writing intrigued you. It was possible he was writing his will; maybe he wanted to disinherit you, leave everything to an orphanage. He could be writing to a mistress, any one of those girls who came by.

It was just getting light when you saw *Hours of June*. You recalled the night he brought it home. Happy because, at last, a poet had written about the most beautiful month of the year. That book in particular bothered you; they all seemed useless, only good for wasting time, but this one made you remember your happy spouse, the husband and lover who recited verses in your ear. All of that was over now, and that trashy book was witness to it: its yellowed pages were the only thing left of that time. But it was the same, it said the same thing as it did forty-five years ago. Furious, you threw it. You were already on your way out, but you thought it over; if he finds the book on the floor, he'll know you came in; he'll lock up and hide the key and you'll never know what he does in the evening. You pick it up and find an envelope that says: "To be opened after my death." You read the line again; that's what it says, no doubt, it's his handwriting. You open it and unfold the page:

> *I will go the night*
> *of the day and month*
> *when I was born:*
> *I will celebrate with my death.*

You look at the calendar, you figure it out, remembering. He wrote it yesterday. Today is the day of that particular night; it's the last day of June. Today is his birthday. You put the sheet of paper in the envelope and put it back where it was. You want to wake him and scream at him by what right does he think he can kill himself. Who is he to leave you abandoned? Doesn't he know that without him you'll die of hunger, cold, and thirst? Does he think you'll go to an old folks' home? You let yourself fall onto the couch. It's true, you think, you weren't mistaken: he's selfish; your fate doesn't matter to him. He only thinks about his own. What will he do today? Will he act the same as always? Will you say something to him? Are you capable of fighting with him? Would you be able to say, "don't do it"? You think of calling the police and accusing him, but of what? And if you did get him locked up, what then? And tomorrow, how will you bury him, who'll come to the wake, how much will it cost? At least you'll save some money on the priest; God doesn't forgive suicides. Besides, he was always an unbeliever, an atheist. He had no catechism other than his books and no god other than himself. You pick up the envelope again. Could he have been joking? And you begin searching, in earnest now, without caring about giving away your presence. You look under the desk, trying to find a pistol, a razor; the weapon he's planning to use to kill himself. All you find is a piece of cheese. Aha! So *this* is where he hides the food! You pick it up to present it to him and complain about his gluttony, but your fingers are smeared with a gelatinous green substance; you smell it, you stare at it. You remain very still. You go back and sit down. Slowly, maliciously, you savor every tiny morsel of the cheese.

NIGHT CALLS
Rafael Pérez Gay

WE ARE INDEBTED TO ANTONIO TABUCCHI, THE ITALIAN WRITER, FOR THE simple but profound notion that life is an appointment. It's just that we do not know with whom, how, where, or when. The key to the enigma involves not so much the answers to these questions as the imagining of different, almost identical worlds. With alternative worlds in mind, one begins to ask one's self what would have occurred if one had done one thing instead of another; what would have happened had we said this and not that. The result would be a world almost identical to this one, yet different, a world in which I, for instance, would not be recounting this history, this tale of blunders.

It was into one of those worlds, almost identical to this very one we inhabit, that Rosaura Márquez and I fell on the day we went to the Gómez's party. More than a party, it was an anthology of humanity. The guests included academics of note, among them our hosts, the Gómezes, writers, painters highly valued on the international market, journalists, psychoanalysts, all meeting to celebrate the age and persistence of one of those invited.

The Gómezes were known to go all out for their parties; they served only the best alcohol and the suppers would have driven any French chef mad with envy.

"This world," a zealous friend was heard to say, "would not be the same without the Gómezes."

He was right. Our world would be almost identical to the one in which we live, only different, without the Gómez's gatherings.

At such a gathering, while one is drinking and talking, a short-lived atmosphere imposes itself, an exceptional air that evokes the vague apprehension that the happiness will melt away like the ice in a glass of carbonated Tehuacan water with whisky. But more than dissolution, the gatherings are like a farewell scene. It's as if the guests at the Gómez's party were gathered in Room B of the Benito Juárez airport to await the arrival of a plane, a voyage, a paradise.

The Gómez's party was in full swing, including the melancholic ambience of those who say farewell in Room B of the airport, when from among one of the circles of conversation, a tall, rapidly balding man made the following pronouncement:

"With one's lover, everyday life disappears. It is what is known as the 'Bovary Effect.'"

Right then I knew I was in the wrong place. For three years I had been carrying on a secret romance with Rosaura, a clandestine affair that created its own stormy and sunny days. In those days we were living a kind of springtime, and the bald man's comment was a dark cloud. I thought the man was about to ask me, "Isn't that how it is with you and Rosaura Márquez?" As a natural result of the anxiety and the whisky, I imagined a monstrous invention, a viewfinder that could, with great visual and verbal precision, reveal people's secrets, the thoughts they could never confess, their dark desires. The bald man did not ask me the question because the videoscope did not exist, and because a beautiful woman who was smoking quite anxiously, answered for me, as though someone had called her by name and number:

"*Madame Bovary* is my favorite novel."

"What is your favorite part?" the bald man asked her.

The woman's breasts bulged under the cloth of her dress, provoking an almost infantile nervousness in the Flaubertian scholar.

"The seduction in the coach," the woman said, raising her cup level with her eyes, as though she had a mouth in her forehead. "The only evidence we have of that erotic encounter is the little pieces of the letter in which she ended her relationship with Rudolphe forever."

"I always tell my students that you do not need three men to suffer what Emma suffers. One is enough for an unforgettable hell." The bald, doctoral Flaubertian was speaking to the woman as though he were about to kiss her on the lips.

"First of all, as Philip Roth has elucidated, there is Rudolphe, passion and ecstasy, an impossible love for the perfect man; then comes Leon, irrepressible, the quotidian lover, practical, love eroded by custom. And, finally," said the bald man as though he himself had just passed through these exhausting phases of adultery, "Charles Bovary, the tyranny of daily life."

I am certain the Flaubertian bald fellow was about to ask the woman, in the presence of the three guests who, along with him and her, formed this particular circle, "Which of these roles do you want me to play in your life?" He did not ask it because a member of our group spoke up, creating a storm:

"I really do like those novels."

The bald man became indignant because the other man had broken the spell he had cast over the woman, who continued her chain-smoking.

"Which novels do you not like?" the bald man asked.

"I don't know," he vacillated for a moment, "Well . . . Musil's. Robert Musil, is it?"

He never should have said such a thing. They almost immolated him on the spot. The bald man and the beautiful woman reproached him for his life, his past, his clothes, and the place where he lived. They threw in his face the names of Lithuanian, Paraguayan, Guatemalan, English, North American, and Chiapanecan novelists; all, according to them, indebted to Robert Musil, children of his blood and his genius. Humanity itself was indebted to the great Austrian writer.

The imprudence of the gentleman who uttered such a barbarous statement caused so great a row that the other guests converged upon him, each hurling a more cutting epithet. One fierce critic could not contain himself and spat in his face before spluttering:

"Garbage!"

The Gómezes are great hosts. To lower the tension they refilled the drinks of the critics and the declarative gentleman, and resorted to mild backslapping in an attempt to reconcile all the literary antagonists:

"Don't be that way; there is no reason to oppose great universal classics."

I retreated from the kangaroo court with my whisky refilled. I thought of my history of three clandestine years with Rosaura and could not avoid asking myself which of the three of Madame Bovary's types of lovers I was for Rosaura. I felt a cramp in the pit of my stomach when I realized that I was none of the three. If I was anyone in the tale, I was Emma Bovary, the hapless lover.

I saw Rosaura approaching, curious about the uproar provoked by the classic novels of all time. I saw her talking to the Gómezes and nodding excitedly in assent, as though they had just given her the keys to their home.

"At last I can see!" she practically screamed at me, as though just recuperating her sight after years of blindness:

"I will undergo psychoanalysis. The Gómezes have suggested it. They say there is no reason why a woman like me should waste her life on a married man."

We were not able to stick to the subject of the Gómez's advice because a hoarse voice asked the guests to be silent. Rosaura told me quietly:

"It's Sarconi, the psychoanalyst. A man of integrity, extremely intelligent, and handsome, besides; maybe I'll let him do my analysis."

"Is he going to give a lecture?" I asked Rosaura.

Sarconi did not expound on the affairs of the soul. It was much better. When the guests quieted down, he raised his voice.

"I shall do magic for you," Sarconi's face lit up like that of a child who has just been granted a wish.

"What kind of magic will he do for us?" the Gómezes asked each other.

I asked myself the same thing. And was Sarconi a real magician? That is, could it be possible that he had anticipated my invention of the monstrous projector, and that it made him able to plumb the depths of the human soul?

In that case, he might give Rosaura and me a therapy session as a couple, during which we would broach such topics as lying, deceit, treachery, jealousy, rivalry, eroticism, and crime.

When Sarconi took out a deck of cards and showed it to the audience, I reconciled with life. Deck in hand, Sarconi addressed the beautiful woman who liked Flaubert and said to her:

"Please draw a card. Show it to your friends and hold on to it."

The woman took the card and pressed it to her breasts like a love letter.

Sarconi shuffled the cards, knit his brow, and spread them out on a table. With the confidence of an expert magician, he drew a single card.

"This is your card: it is the ace of hearts."

The woman lit a cigarette before answering. With a gesture comparable only to that of Emma Bovary as she takes the lethal poison, she said:

"I am sorry, but I have the four of spades."

The audience uttered a unanimous groan, as when a soccer player misses a free kick at a wide-open goal.

Sarconi was disconcerted, but he recovered with the alacrity of a professional accustomed to failure:

"Nothing is infallible in these times, my lady friend, not even magic."

I overheard one of the guests saying:

"Listen, Norma, this man is a genius. He has actually performed an instant psychoanalysis right before our very eyes. What he was trying to say to the woman is that she will never win at love, which is what the suit of hearts represents; on the contrary, in her future there will be only sentimental misfortune, which is what the spades represent."

"I agree," I said to the exegete of failed magic.

Sarconi did not give up. From his pockets he took three small colored tumblers and a little white ball, which he held up between his index finger and thumb. He challenged his audience:

"Where will the little ball be?"

Of course no one could tell where the little ball ended up. Sarconi was happy, and happiness attracts success. Minutes later he quite cleanly extracted three silk scarves and a coin from the ear of the beautiful woman. His act was greeted with great applause from the audience, but the night was leaning toward tragedy: a bald man who pontificates concerning adultery, an unsolicited lecture on Flaubert, an unfortunate reader of Musil, and as if that were not enough, a psychoanalyst who desired with all his might to be a magician. But the night when Rosaura and I fell into one of those worlds almost identical to this one, as proposed by Tabucchi's enigma, was not yet over.

Chance is capable of anything. We said good-bye to the Gómezes at two o'clock in the morning, thanking them for their hospitality, the whisky, and the affection with which we were treated. On our way out, as Rosaura bade Sarconi good-bye, I heard him say to her:

"Don't forget to call me."

Unknowingly, we had fallen into another of those worlds that appear to be like this one, but are essentially different. On the way to Rosaura's apartment, a car pulled up next to us at a stoplight, and the people inside greeted us with an exaggerated ardor, given the late hour. I said:

"Did you see who that was? Amelia and her friends. She's more of a gossip than Flaubert. Our secret is shot to hell."

"What secret? Everybody knows. What a mess. You made fun of everyone all night long."

"That's a lie," I said to her, "They made fun of me. They all invented fake professions, imaginary lives."

The reproaches reached back to long-past times and places. I heard myself saying to Rosaura:

"Hey, that happened at Christmas two years ago."

"Yes, but I got left all alone because you were with your family."

"Please forget about that."

"And the thing with the dog, do I have to forget that, too?"

"I've told you a thousand times that I did not kill Patan, he died of old age. For God's sake!"

"You swore to me that you'd take care of him while I was in Zacatecas," Rosaura recalled. "And when I returned, what did I find? Patan's grave."

"I didn't kill anyone. On the other hand, all during Holy Week you kept calling my home at two in the morning and hanging up."

"Night calls," Rosaura responded apologetically. "I was beside myself, overpowered by jealousy."

With incredibly destructive efficiency we dredged the river of our amorous wretchedness until Rosaura said to me:

"This is where I get off."

Despair takes on incredible forms. One of those forms was the sinister promise that Rosaura made me. She swore to return all my belongings she had accumulated in a box: postcards, books, clothes left over from happy nights, pens, letters so sentimental you would cry reading them. This was what she vowed. The sinister part was the manner in which she would return the box. She would personally deliver it to the door of my home. If the Virgin of Guadalupe herself had told me that she was coming to dinner at my house in person, it would not have caused me as much consternation as that promise.

I wandered about the city all night. I had the ingenuous idea that we all go forward at dawn, riding in a car, toward places unknown. Suddenly I was thirsty, not for alcohol, as you would expect from a desperate man, but for water. I went into a VIPs and ordered coffee and a Tehuacan water. They wreaked incredible havoc in my stomach. I pulled a napkin out of a dispenser and tore off a piece. I rolled it into a little wad and said to myself, "If it goes into the cup of coffee, she'll deliver the box; if it doesn't, she won't." I took careful aim, and let the little ball fly.

I'll save the melancholy, that territory of lost orgasms, memory, and other forms of blackmail with which people long for other people. I will spare you for two reasons: first, because that time was, precisely, in a world almost identical to this one, a world only slightly different from this one, in which there was no Rosaura, and second, because I want to take this story all the way to the day when the Gómezes, who are generous friends and great hosts, invited Rosaura and me to one of their gatherings, this time each of us individually.

It was the rainy season and the city went mad, as it does every year, under a sky of rare shades of blue and orange at twilight. At the party, in a remote corner of a room, I found Rosaura:

"How's life treating you?" I asked.

"Well," she responded, "I live alone. I do what I want. I eat when I want, and I don't wash dirty shirts or go to the cleaners to pick up clothes."

Life treats everyone, or almost everyone, badly. That is why I knew she was not living alone. She insisted:

"So many things have happened, no?"

"Yeah, so many, and thanks a lot for that last thing," I said with shameful lack of refinement.

"I have my list of basic principles."

"What does your list say?"

"Never do anything just to hurt someone. It doesn't work. I'm leaving," she said, "someone's waiting for me."

"Who's waiting for you?" I finally asked.

"Sarconi. I live with him. Didn't you know?"

"The magician," I managed to say to her through the May rain, in a world almost identical to this one.

HE WOULDN'T GIVE UP HIS TURN
Humberto Rivas

HE NOTICED THEY HAD SURROUNDED THE GUY WHILE HE WAS MAKING HIS phone call. He wondered if it was an international call. He wanted to make a call too, across the border; he would surely wake up Anne, in the middle of the night in her country so far to the north.

They were shaved nearly bald. Military dog tags hung from their necks. One of them, the one who moved most slowly, the one with his eyes nearly shut, was trying to see the tiny screen that displays the cost of the call. They guy making the call turned to look at the person crowding him. The others laughed like idiots. One of the gang, a guy with a long, curved nose, was rocking a doll in his arms. It was some kind of stuffed bird with a curved beak (he thought it resembled the kid carrying it), a cockscomb, and talons. When you squeezed its body, it spoke. You couldn't understand what it said.

The other two kept on laughing and crowding the guy using the phone, who was apparently speaking English. The one carrying a telephone card was dancing to the rhythm of the metro loudspeakers.

He kept waiting. He wasn't going to let them have his place in line. He would make his call before they did. They performed all kinds of contortions, and laughed. He fixed his gaze on the television screen next to the telephones; inside a small restaurant: they were showing *Secrets* by Judith Krantz, and at that moment Nicky, a very beautiful actress, appeared on screen in a light blue miniskirt, showing off her fantastic legs; he almost got an erection and wished he were at home so he could check her out at ease. Just the same, he imagined himself being intimate with her, caressing her silk stockings. . . . For a few minutes he forgot about Anne.

One of the young savages hit the doll; another grabbed it from him, hitting the hitter. Low blow, as they say in boxing. The one who had rescued the doll bent over with laughter and asked the aggressor why he had treated the animal that way. The aggressor said because it was ugly.

They reeked of alcohol and marijuana. They with their madness and he with his, he thought, and Anne asleep, who knows if alone, and here he was, punishing his heart and wretchedly spending the little money he had saved making these calls, so late at night and tired, with his eyes bloodshot, as red as a communist flag, so maligned these days. Finally, one of them touched the man on the shoulder and the latter turned around and started screaming insults in a language that sounded like English from Australia.

It happened lightning fast. The three of them began beating on the man with precise karate blows. The police avoided the scene. A few passengers saw the fight and backed away frightened. They didn't want to intervene either. He noticed their mascot on the floor, picked it up, and let out a loud scream. The young savages stopped, raised their bald heads, and fixed their gaze on him. He raised the filthy doll and threatened to gut it. Everything got quiet, except the loudspeakers that kept on talking in their nasal Cuban twang.

They let go of the man who, seeing that he was free, ran out of the station, gasping and scattering his belongings on the floor. The three laughed and approached him. He wielded the idiotic doll. Seeing them closing in, he thought he had no alternative. Before they attacked, he began tearing the bird apart; he ripped it open as the skinheads cried out. A foul-smelling, yellowish liquid ran down his hands; he smeared it on the face of the nearest one. With his boots, he stomped on what was left of the torn doll and planted a well-placed kick on the testicles of another before he could attack. They picked up what was left of their detestable toy and left the station howling.

The police were watching him over their shoulders. The station began emptying. With his hands smeared with the crap that seemed like yellowish blood to him, he dialed Anne's number from memory.

A male voice answered. He asked for her. Just a minute, said the man and almost immediately, he heard Anne's voice, somewhat hoarse. Anne of the green eyes, in his arms. Anne so warm, asking him not to go to that horrible country, and he saying that he feared his own more, that his own country disgusted him even worse, that there were even more maniacs there. . . . "You shouldn't call in the middle of the night," she said, "We were sleeping," and he wanted to get his hands on them . . . unable to adapt to his country again. He detested and desired her so much at that moment. I'm not going to have an abortion, she said, I won't abort and I don't want to see you for now . . .

A hand on his neck, a cold, rough hand: the young savages had returned with reinforcements. They had returned to avenge an offense to their sullied honor, to their honor as slaves, as people who are promised everything and never granted anything: somewhat like what was happening to him with Anne.

They had multiplied, and it looked like the police were backing them too. They raised high the pelt of their idiotic bird and let out war whoops, like the Apaches in the movies. Oh, how I despise you, Anne, he was able to say before dropping the receiver and facing the wild gang. He fixed his gaze on one of them; his eyes burned like hot coals and he had feathers in his mouth; he yelled and spit up a green, then yellow, then purple substance.

He managed to prop himself up against the wall before feeling the first blows. He screamed at Anne through the receiver hanging there, that she was the same as that gang of cretins.

He never found out if the laughter he heard came from the receiver or from the skinheads. He saw red and blue lights and flashes. He couldn't tell if it was the police, an ambulance, photographers . . .

THE BASILISK
Daniel Sada

PRECIOUS, BETTER YET, AGGRESSIVE, THE BROWN SERPENT SLITHERS SOUND-lessly through the brambles, in the empty lot out back, over there where no one goes; ominous, fearless, she's probably looking for the ideal hiding place, or trying to show off, in all her great length, to any pair of eyes gazing at her.

It is the astonished child who sees her!

She looks like the root of a century-old tree that has magically come to life. Vain, deceitful, she advances toward the ideal space in which her meandering movements and her color can blend into the undergrowth. And the boy takes off running, wailing against the wind, trying to sound a warning, but where are his parents? His howls grow louder. No matter that he searches the rooms anxiously for them or opens a window to the street to see if they are coming. There is no sign of them. Whom does he expect to see? At this blazing hour there is no one on the street, and no amount of yelling will make a bit of difference. Now then, he must calm down and control his reaction. He tries not to imagine that fiendish countenance right in his face, jaws agape, acid fangs ready to strike. He tries not to imagine the lethal bite, the uncontrollable spurt that would blot out everything. It is better that he sleep, that he let his dreams carry him away.

And the snake goes on . . . ! I wish I could see her again!

When the parents come home, they see their boy under the covers at around four in the afternoon, or rather, they see a bundle and they poke it, then uncover it. He is awake, trying to say something through his sobbing. From where I am, all I have to do to get the picture is hear the voices of the people caught up in that situation. There is bickering and scolding, and everything is dismal now, while I'm on pins and needles.

On various occasions there have been scenes like this in this home: the boy insisting on the improbable things he believes, and the father creating a commotion, angrily denying such hallucinations; they're mistaken notions, fantastic quandaries: whether it be that the rain is always talking to the earth or that a silver star fell right into the backyard, a star as tiny as a coin, still vibrating and shining, or that the night wind sometimes sings. . . . Whimsy, improvisations, perhaps approximations to what could be: but this time it's different.

"What do you mean, a snake six feet long?"

Declaring, "That just isn't possible!" the father proclaims his disbelief, and the mother seconds him by simply nodding. The boy's reasons are to no avail, his impatience merely bewilders them. The glimmer of intelligence in his sparkling eyes is enough to make his father send him to his room. . . . Wary, frantic, the boy goes.

But his mother gathers that there is something strange going on; being a woman, she has a hunch, and since she is open to superstition, after a while, with the excuse of going to the bathroom, she secretly takes her son some sugar to alleviate his fear. Just in case. . . .

Then:

"And you really, truly saw it?"

The boy just cries, he can't answer, and what's more, now he's afraid to fall into a trap. From where I am, I believe I detect a hardening of his position. The atmosphere is drowning in moving shadows, making all colors blend into one: an intense sepia tint pervades the room, there is an annoying sound moving about: what could it be? An absent presence. Suddenly the mother decides not to ask any more questions. Then she leaves, confused. She feels that the bedroom in which her husband is waiting is suddenly very far away. She walks, then runs. . . . She finally gets there, out of breath.

There are deliberations. Of the many outbursts that have erupted in this home because of the boy's imaginings, none has alarmed them so much that the father has felt obliged to investigate; he tends more toward laziness than toward denial, and he waits, he simply waits, to see what happens. . . . It is also taken for granted that to date, nothing out of the ordinary has actually occurred. One of the parents has to take the responsibility. . . . As a matter of fact, if it happens at night, the father will immediately have to search the backyard thoroughly, making noise, carrying a light and a pistol. He will have to confront those phantasms—be they good or evil. He will have to shoot them. Let us see how he does. The fact is that today the boy did not see pretty things, but rather a snake, about whose beauty very few have written, for it is the line that flees, long, almost invisible. What is disconcerting is the idea that it disappears and that it schemes to do so. Could what the boy has perceived be real?

From where I am everything appears plain.

During their discussion—over in their bedroom—the mother alludes to the popular belief that when a snake comes into a house, it is an unequivocal sign of the existence of a monstrosity there. It is what is roughly called a "psychic event," "*mandinga*" or the "evil eye," but no ones knows what it really is. In the meantime, the father strikes a match, takes out his cigarette, and lights it; he breathes out a puff of smoke, thinking he'll solve the problem by walking around the room.

More likely the causes are altogether different. More likely the father would rather conclude that the child creates fantasies because he has no siblings. Will they have to provide him one to break the curse? Around his classmates he hunkers down, won't play, loses spontaneity; he won't take a risk. . . . In a way his loneliness is always a victory; it is the perpetual magic that by dint of exaggeration has become a reality.

And the serpent is still seeking refuge. . . . The boy is asleep, he seems impervious. He is probably on a voyage toward a unique form.

The clock. Over there, far away.

Exhausting tick-tock.

Like this: the parents feel a certain discomfort as they discern their mistakes. As soon as, with lukewarm pretense, they exhibit their errors, they acrimoniously shift their guilt to each other, and their tone of voice now begins to transform into a macabre echo; they feel, they must be feeling it more and more, that there is a horrendous power around them that wants to expel them from their bedroom; an enigmatic sweat appears on their faces, their bodies tremble, their tongues strangle them. Anguish! Magic! Or what? It isn't that big a deal; there's only a persistent gloom, a certain excrescence that passes through walls. Then the couple join hands, leave—which they must any way they can—and go down the hall that leads to the rest of the house; the trek turns out to be an eternity for them, and although it isn't far, they arrive at the dining room very tired; finally there, it appears larger to them, all of a sudden it's like a storehouse of moving shadows that first delineate and then blur what is there, and yes, what was there: the usual furnishings. What they suddenly notice is that the grandfather clock perched on the back wall has lost a hand.

They have to get closer to see if it is true. Which they do, step by step, holding each other's hand. Their fear is palpable, and actually in rhythm with the dramatic, useless tick-tock, as though it were a warning of an unreal outcome; thus, it is uncertainty, raging uncertainty, that is traipsing around erasing the contours of things; it is appearance—perhaps personified appearance— who opens the windows letting the wind blow in freely. And with the same vehemence and the same fear the boy had felt a few hours ago, the couple want to go and look for it, but the light is going out. Where? In the dark, the couple can only hug each other. It is now they sense the cursed animal moving about in the dining room, under the table, zig-zagging and inconspicuous, he's coming right at them. . . . No!

Neither one of them can avoid it; they have to resign themselves. In their immobility, in the darkness that enlarges or reduces uncertain spaces, they will have to remain, however long it takes, dumbfounded, waiting paralyzed by fear for the light to return. Never! A long time goes by and all they hear is the wind snaking ahead: outside, inside, unexpectedly, the two hear the diffuse tick-tock sounding a bland contrast to their palpitations. It would also seem that it could all stop at any moment and, having finished its job, the rude serpent, in all its great length, might leave the house. Nevertheless, in an elusive turn, the splendor of the moon appears in the distance.

Beyond the window the picture is vague, a useless clarity, provoking, disorienting. With the light coming in, the light of a match would be ineffectual, although it might be better, since with the incipient flame, the husband could scare off the stubborn vipers that have been gathering around. Conscious of this, the man desperately searches his clothes but cannot find the box of matches, bah! he's left it in the bedroom, what's the use! all he finds are his cigarettes, which can't do any good now. Thus, impelled by something undefined, the couple begin moving forward, hugging each other, in the wrong direction: toward their son's room, perhaps too far away; a dark route where the consequences could be more precise. But the child is not crying, isn't calling them, isn't crying out in pain, yes, he's sleeping, but how?

There is an insurmountable, imaginary wall. There is an impediment. And what's more, the struggle to get beyond whatever it is quickly becomes an inability to act: the couple quits trying. Nevertheless, they let themselves be attracted by the handful of lights outside. Although there are many windows, one is especially inviting, and they go toward it: like mindless blobs.

It is a short walk. They get there. It is the bathroom, smelling of *immortelles*, and the strange thing is that they are not in the habit of putting flowers in the house; just the same, the aroma calms them. That is why they intuit that this tight space is the only place they will be safe all night, safe, from who knows what? because they observe with childlike eyes that there is a magnetic light around the tops of the trees and the rest is a blur, except for the sky, from which the stars seem to be tearing loose.

The father does not believe it, cannot accept it; in order to do so, he would have to accept as fact that he made a mistake when he scolded his son for going around inventing what would never be a peaceful subject between them, there are too many explanations, and he covers his eyes. . . . But the mother remains speechless, she succumbs to fantasy, giving herself over to what could be a never-ending show. Granules of light come down; the moon is falling apart! and a rain shower drums down. A symbolic sprinkling that she could avoid if she does as her husband has done, but she is too far gone. . . .The darkness is escaping through a hole in the wall! . . . She will be hypnotized if she lets herself be attracted by all that. The husband knowingly pulls her by her left wrist: *Better squat down and cover your eyes like me, or just close them. . . .* She comes out of it, but not quite: what is happening outside is to be celebrated. In a while you can see the two of them, lying facedown, like rag dolls. There they must remain until dawn, without moving, defenseless, truly resigned to the worst, without sleeping, they won't be able to.

Are death and its apparatus prowling about?

A movie made only for me; nevertheless, from where I am, something becomes disconnected . . .

The henhouse rises, is forced to rise, to become lost in clouds of dust, but they do not see it. The wind is now singing a lullaby, but they do not hear it. All they can hear is the sound of breaking windows, perhaps from the dining room, and the prolonged screeching of wood and pieces of the ceiling coming down. The father, still in character, covers his ears and, although he tries not to, he falls prey to terror.

It is probable that when dawn breaks the husband will hurry to the backyard to learn point by point what happened during the night, and that he will use these facts to give the lie to his son, and thus to his wife. It is probable that he will carry a gun, since—and it is now time to say it—what has actually been bothering him is not getting to sleep in his own bed. Regardless, in or out of their dreams, things keep on happening. . . . It is in the morning that the rooster, rustic announcer perched on a grapevine, lets out an all too-strident cocka-doodle-doo, followed by three more that echo each other and perturb the couple. They stand up, anxious to find out if all the disorder actually took place, or was just their imagination. Day brings other things: the night noises have disappeared. Contrary to what happened, they see all the objects are in order, just like before: the dining room, the parlor, the clock perched on the wall, with both hands indicating the time, exactly.

The spouses look at each other. In their faces are signs of affliction. Then, by inertia, they move toward their son's room, hoping against hope that, since he has not cried out, the snake has not attacked him, and that he has not been lying dead for the last few hours. Actually, they can move as fast as they want, since there are no more obstructions. They open the door and what they see is logical: the child is awake, playing with his toy cars on the floor, talking to himself as he always does. The father, getting right to the point, asks him a question:

"Tell me again, where was that snake you saw?"

"In the yard, out back. It was about six feet long!"

"Come. Hurry. You can go on playing later."

The three of them go outside.

Of course, because he is in a rush, the father forgets his favorite weapon, the one he has used in the most compromising situations. But the mother, who is plenty careful, opens her kitchen closet and in a matter of seconds takes out a big knife. Lucky for them, they find the snake—very long, unbelievably longer than they thought—lying dead a few steps from the well.

"We have to get it off the grounds right away," says the terrified father.

But he has to take the initiative. Who, if not he? He has to be bold to grab it and go—he does it quickly, looping it round and round like a lariat—toward the nearest wall. Mother and son contemplate the maneuver, tense but happy. There she goes; the snake in the air is the line that twists and turns: it will disappear.

The prophesies have come true.

From where I am, I see that in the brambles yellow flowers have blossomed.

The father, dismayed, walks back slowly. When he reaches his son, he is unable to utter a single word; he looks at him with reluctance, but not with contrition; thus, all he can do is stretch out his hand and lovingly stroke his head. . . . Of course, if the boy someday gets it into that head to say that he has seen a plague of vipers in the backyard, his father will undoubtedly have to believe him, not to mention his mother.

And I? I wonder what I could say?

SCHEHERESADE
Rosa Beltrán

I HAVE A LOVER TWENTY-FOUR YEARS OLDER THAN I AM WHO HAS TAUGHT ME two things. One, that there can be no true passion if one does not cross some limit, and two, that an older man can only offer you his money or his sympathy. Rex does not give me money or sympathy. That is why he says that our passion, which has transcended limits, is in danger of beginning to extinguish itself at any moment.

First Night

Before meeting him, I had attended two book presentations and nothing had ever happened, which is just so many words, because actually it's when nothing happens that things are really happening. And that time they happened as follows: I was alone, in the middle of a crowded room, asking myself why I had decided to torture myself that way, when I realized that Rex, a famous writer I knew only by name, was seated next to me. When the first participant's reading was over, I applauded. Next thing I knew, Rex raised his hand, rebuked the participant, and took his seat once again. With very few variations, this was the dynamic of that presentation: papers were read, followed by applause, and Rex either praised or destroyed the speaker, always commenting with quotes from one of the Great Figures he kept handy.

Someone read, Rex criticized, another read, Rex criticized, I applauded. If minimalism *is* foresight and the reduction of elements to their lowest possible number of variables, this was the most minimalist presentation I had ever been to. The penultimate presentation by a feminist author having ended, Rex criticized, I applauded and went to the ladies' room. I heard him say that human stupidity could sink no lower. When I got back, before the event had ended, I noticed that Rex had his hand on my chair and was distractedly conversing with someone. When I pointed to the place where I'd been sitting—and which his autonomous, palpitating hand now guarded like a crab—Rex looked me in the eye and said, "I put it there to keep it warm." Two hours later we were making love, frantically. That's what they say: "frantically." Also: "madly." In love, borrowed phrases are everything, and you can never be sure of saying what you want when you love. But, when you want with all your might not to be there and cannot do it, what do you say then?

Third Night

The first thing I must admit is that I don't know very well what nihilistic decadence consists of, because before meeting Rex I had not thought about it. According to him, the term defines Generation X, the most decadent and luckless generation of this century, to which I unfortunately belong. But if I wanted to follow the plan of action I should follow according to Rex, I could only regret one act: having sat next to him, such a famous writer, at a book presentation. The golden rule among people who attend this kind of event is that no one should get involved with anyone else, and that friendships, if any should develop, should be based upon the purest self-interest (I give you, you give me; I introduce you, you introduce me; I read you, you read me), or total disregard. Rex says that any relationship that isn't a result of alcohol is false.

Seventh Night

Today Rex and I decided on something quite original: that no two people have ever loved each other the way we do. And to confirm it, we used the phrases all lovers use. One single being in two different bodies. Twin souls amidst a multitude of strangers. A hundred different vaginas and only one real cunt.

Tenth Night

This had been going on since the first time, but I had forgotten to mention it. We were in the climactic moment, making love frantically, as I have said, and suddenly the room was full of visitors. The first to arrive was She of the Extremely Narrow Waist. Rex began talking about this old lover of his because my posture reminded him of her. She was decisive, ardent, and a brunette. You had to grasp her tightly by the waist because if not she was likely to fall off. "Like this," he said, squeezing me. "Oh, how that woman could move up and down," he added, while holding on to me, nostalgic. But after a while, he pointed his index finger and warned me:

"Many may imitate her, but no one can equal her, no one."

And, sunk in this reflection, he went to pour himself a whiskey. After a few minutes during which I, who had also lapsed into a kind of dream state, was pondering the great passion between Rex and me, he broke the silence:

"She could squat perfectly," he said, referring to that other woman, "Look, I get goose bumps when I remember it."

It was true: the sickly white skin, untouched by the sun for years, had little pointy lumps all over it.

"Like a flesh piston," he said, as if in a trance, "up and down, beside herself, over me, emitting impeccable cries."

According to Rex, that squatting woman's performance art was excellent. She made him reach the heavens, without any exaggeration, six times. The very day she gave herself to him, before leaving, She of the Extremely Narrow Waist asked him to make love to her from behind.

"She wanted to make me an offering," Rex explained, "a gift."

After this confession, which seemed quite strange to me, there was another silence. I thought Rex's story was an indirect way of asking me for something, so I wrapped my arms around a pillow and offered myself, on my hands and knees, with my back to him. "Don't move," he said, and in a few seconds I saw a camera flash. I waited a bit longer, but nothing happened, and after a few anxious moments, I heard someone next to me snoring.

Night 69

"Why do I like it so much when you talk to me about your old lovers?" I lied.

"Because the flesh *is* history," Rex explained, quite serious, "although this is understood by very few people."

And then, very close to my ear, he whispered:

"Flesh for flesh's sake does not exist."

Night 104

Two weeks later, he brought me the photo. Along with a letter that said, "I adore the dark star of your forehead, but I adore a thousand times more the other one, the shameless one, that bottomless abyss that unites us." All the rest was interminable praise: of my breasts, whiter and more beautiful than those of Venus; of my buttocks, as round and full as those in Ingres's paintings; of my thighs, my perfect back and belly. Of each centimeter of my body, always in comparison with other women. Never had anyone been more beautiful than me: none of the lips, navels, hair, nor long necks that preceded me could compete with me, according to Rex. Freud says that in every sexual relationship there are at least four people sharing the bed. In our case there were at least twenty. Or thirty. At least that's what I thought at first. Little by little I began realizing that if Rex's ex-lovers had been crammed into the room, we would have had to leave for lack of space.

"Wouldn't it be better if we used a condom?" I suggested.

Rex's refusal was categorical:

"What would have come of the Great Lovers of History if they had messed with such petty things?" he said.

He immediately got out of bed, dressed and left, slamming the door.

Night 386

For some reason, I feel obliged to declare that I enjoyed a happy childhood, that my father loved me a lot and that he was *not* a macho dog. Or maybe he was, maybe he was as macho as others. But this has nothing to do with Rex and me. What's wrong between him and me is simply a matter of polarity: men bore me, as they do all the women of my generation, which as I have stated, is called Gen X. This I have been able to prove. "Political correctness" is nothing more than a kind of cynical hypocrisy. It is the pretension to asepsis on the gloves of the surgeon who uses a rusty scalpel, and the world is not an operating room.

Night 514

At night, after we part, Rex puts my name under his tongue. He keeps it there all night, like a chocolate kiss. For me, on the other hand, his gestures become fuzzy, his hands, his body over mine disappear. I can only remember his voice. Like a movie I saw in which the characters date by telephone without ever meeting, Rex has become an audio person, incorporeal. Rex is the shape of his words. And his words, the love inspired in him by the women who came before me.

Night 702

Yesterday he brought more women into the room. Their names surprise me more than they do, they make me imagine a thousand and one possibilities. She Who Cried over Cioran; Scorpion Woman; The Immutable Beloved; The Wild Nun. Each with a very specific history and way of making love.

"My women have always been willful," says Rex. "They have known how to choose their positions. On top, or cross-legged, on their side, each according to her taste and preference."

My unspoken role was to imitate them. And what is more, to surpass them. If I improvised some gesture, Rex would subtly move me into one of their poses. The Lady of Ancient Lineage, for example, very upright on top of him, casting her disdainful gaze upon the world, and he would tell me her story. I never learned their real names.

"It's out of respect," Rex said, "to avoid running into them on the street some day."

One afternoon, while making love, I made the slightest hint at improvisation, and as I began kissing him, following the road from groin to eyelids, he compared me to Eve. "The first woman," I thought proudly, and in response, I walked all around the room before Jehovah arrived and chased me out of paradise.

Night 996

I had lost count of how often we met, given the relative manner in which time had begun to elapse and, as you would expect, Rex's whims had multiplied. To accomplish them he began postponing his trips and lectures, which was not an inconsiderable gesture given the money he earned, or rather, didn't earn because of seeing me. He invented more and more unrealistic pretexts to cancel his appointments, to stay far from his family, and began exercising his amatory functions much like a runner on the stock market on Wall Street, on time and implacable. I was his lover, he said, it was because of me. What could I do but respond to such dedication with matching fervor? Suddenly I was obliged to surpass the squatting of She of the Extremely Narrow Waist, keeping my legs in the air for hours like Scorpion Woman, perfecting the timing of The Frog, or remaining perfectly still on my side, like Singing Spoonful. Most often, no matter how tired I was, I had to move frantically, my hair waving in the wind like Yesterday's Medusa, the lover whom he had the hardest time forgetting. Along with my erotic gymnastics, I had to go hungry for hours, even whole days, pale and with dark rings under my eyes, sustained only by the saying of Chateaubriand that the True Lover must resist all assaults like a city in ruins. As if this weren't enough, one day when we had made love for hours, not to mention that this had gone on for days, Rex decided to turn on the television in the hotel room where we met. I got scared to death when I noted the stoicism with which Sharon Stone, totally nude and perched upon her lover, put a tie around her neck and without missing a beat, held her breath as he, lost in the purest pleasure, strangled her as they performed coitus.

"Leave it there," said Rex, pouring himself a whiskey, "don't you dare change it."

And looking at me knowingly:

"That's how we can come up with some new ideas."

I got up with difficulty, and painfully walked to the minibar. He explained what he would do to me when I got into the tub, when I bent over, trying, uselessly, to dress, when hours later, I would fall asleep. "There'll be no timeouts," he warned.

I took out a Coca Cola and put it next to my ear: inside I could hear the virtual bombardment of an imaginary city.

Night 1000 and One

Yesterday afternoon, I tried to give him an ultimatum: them or me. It was a moment of despair, I admit. I was fed up with competing with other women. I wanted to be loved for myself. "But you encompass them all!" Rex said to me, moved. At times like that I feel I can't let him down. The worst thing that can happen is that tomorrow will come (which is the only thing I desire) and that I, being solicitous, will be obliged to surpass the pleasure of the preceding nights. The next worst thing is that, his repertory used up, Rex will see me as I am and decide that the moment (fatal) has arrived for me to become part of his inventory.

THE BIG BRUSH
David Toscana

THE STREET WAS TOO DESERTED FOR MIDMORNING. RUBÉN RUSHED TO PUT the key in the door because the phone was ringing. As soon as he got it open he stretched toward the receiver on the counter.

"*The Big Brush* at your service."

"Sorry," said the voice at the other end, "wrong number."

He hung up. Since his business had taken a downturn, his fantasies had made him imagine that every phone call could be the solution: a million-dollar job, a contract to paint a thousand houses or the white line down a new cross-country road, a furniture factory in dire need of lacquer, the transit authority having decided to paint all the no-parking zones yellow.

His creditors, on the other hand, never called. To do that would have been to warn their prey and give him time to run or hide. Only the roar of their motorcycles announced their presence, when they were almost right there. They were all the same, whether sent by the bank, the suppliers, the tax office, or the landlord. They wore white shirts with three open buttons, so sheer that the slightest perspiration was enough to reveal chest hairs and nipples. They all seemed to drive the same bikes, carry their papers in the same navy-blue saddle bags, and wear the same imitation Ray-Ban sunglasses.

One had visited him two hours before.

"Mr. Rubén Soto?"

And Rubén answered they way he answered all of them:

"He's not in right now. Is there a message?"

"I'm from Pimsa. Tell him if he doesn't pay by Friday his account will be referred to the legal department."

"Okay, I'll tell him."

Two months before, he'd had the help of an employee, which let him keep the business open from eight in the morning to eight at night. Now he closed whenever he had to go home or to the bank or on any kind of errand. And whether he was gone for five minutes or a whole shift, the sign on the door was the same: BACK SOON. A sign almost no one read.

"Mundo," he told him the day he let him go, "I don't have money to pay you."

"I know," said Mundo, "you haven't paid me for two months."

During that time Mundo had never asked for his pay. He had become accustomed to thinking of Rubén not as a boss, but as a friend, since there was so much free time that he rarely received an order from him. Instead, they passed the time talking, playing cards, and inventing ways to get through the workday.

In a fit of scruples, after Mundo had already packed his things, Rubén added:

"I promise you that when things get better I'll pay you your two months and your severance pay."

But there was no reason to believe things would improve.

"Don't you worry, sir. After all, I'm not supporting anyone."

"And if you care to," said Rubén, "you can come back to work with me again."

Mundo did not respond. He crossed the street and sat on the curb. In a few minutes a shuttle cab stopped. When Rubén saw it leave and fade in the distance, he wished from the bottom of his heart that he could leave just as Mundo had.

The telephone rang again. The voice he heard at the other end of the line was more disappointing than the wrong number. It was Clara, his wife, and Clara never called for happy reasons.

"Rube?"

"Yeah, what?"

"I have bad news for you."

He kept silent. The tricks his wife employed to begin a conversation instead of getting right to the point bored him.

"Aren't you going to ask me what it is?"

Rubén supposed it had to do with money. What else would Clara be thinking about? Then he thought that maybe Aunt Encarna had finally died, but she would not consider that bad news.

"You don't care about what happens to us," Clara complained.

"Yeah, well," said Rubén to avoid a discussion, "tell me what's the matter. Clara had now changed her mind.

"Not right now, I'll tell you when you get home."

"Whatever, but I have to hang up; I have a customer."

Usually that phrase was a trick to end conversations. This time there actually was a lady in the doorway, with a competing brand's color sampler in hand.

"Listen," said the woman, "do you carry Berel brand paint?"

Rubén was fed up with that question. Everyone who came in the door wanted Berel paint and not the crap he sold.

"No, ma'am, I only carry Cope."

The woman was doing an about-face when Rubén delivered his well-rehearsed line:

"Cope offers you the same quality at half the price."

Rubén's hands trembled from the thunder of an approaching motorcycle. The woman stood still while she mulled over the intentions of the man behind the counter.

"You guarantee it?"

Rubén nodded assent, relieved. The motorcycle had passed by.

"Look," the woman said pointing to the sampler, "I want three gallons of a color like this."

Now he needed to surmount the second obstacle. Berel came in thirty-six colors, Cope in only twelve. Rubén could not sell her that color. The people at Cope are assholes, he thought, they don't realize that only eggs sell by the dozen. While he was planning his strategy, he noticed that the woman was checking out the place more carefully. There were no gallon cans of paint to be seen anywhere, just an occasional shelf with half-liter cans. On the wall, a metal sign read PAINT YOUR VICTORY WITH VICTORY BRUSHES. There were only two three-inch brushes hanging on the display. The few sheets of sandpaper were curling from the dampness, and the floor sported a coat of dust from at least two weeks of not having been swept.

"A lot of people complain about that color," said Rubén, "because once you apply it, it looks a lot darker."

There was a touch of vulnerability in his voice that inspired trust. The woman asked:

"Well, then what would you recommend?"

Rubén took out his sampler and pointed to one of the colors.

"You'd be better off with the Walnut Brown."

"I don't know," said the woman, "I wanted something a bit more yellow."

"Yellow tones end up tiring your eyes."

He congratulated himself on his response, only regretting he had not thought of it sooner. It seemed an effective way to dissuade anyone, and it could be used for any color.

"Do you have it in stock?"

"Why do you ask, ma'am?"

"It's just that your store seems so empty . . ."

Rubén smiled.

"I'd rather keep everything in the stockroom," and he pointed behind himself, to the door covered with a curtain.

He turned around and yelled:

"Mundo, bring me three gallons of Walnut Brown!"

"Wait," said the woman, "you haven't told me the price yet."

"For all three, or each one?"

"The total."

Rubén opened a drawer and took out the price list. He hated to open it because it made him see the pile of overdue bills. Only the phone bill had "Paid" stamped on it.

"Do you need brushes or rollers?"

The woman shook her head. She didn't seem as docile as a minute before.

"Mundo!" he called again.

The telephone started to ring. One, two, three times, and still Rubén did not move or take his eyes off the price list. On a piece of cardboard he began writing lists of numbers as they came randomly to mind. First, the year of his birth, then the last paycheck he had gotten a long time ago, when he worked in a refrigerator factory. The third was his zip code. The telephone was insistent. For Rubén, more than five rings was bad manners and there had been eleven to that moment. The woman moved toward the phone, as if to answer it. Finally, she said:

"Hey, aren't you going to answer?"

Rubén was sure it was Clara. She probably couldn't resist the urge to tell him the bad news and, of course, to ask him if the customer had bought anything.

"No," said Rubén, "I give preference to the people who bother to come in, not to those who just dial a number."

It rang fourteen times, then went silent. Rubén put the list back in the drawer.

"I don't know what's wrong with this kid. He's probably in the back of the stockroom and can't hear me."

He asked the woman to wait and went behind the curtain. The so-called stockroom was a little room with a desk and a toilet. There was a pile of burlap cloth and a crate full of empty bottles, mostly tequila bottles, in which he dispensed thinner. That's all. The closest thing to Mundo was a Dallas Cowboys T-shirt with number eighty on it, hanging from a nail on the wall; his work shirt that he had decided to leave behind because, as a matter of fact, he no longer had work. Rubén looked at his watch, measuring the woman's patience. He didn't have to wait very long. Before two minutes were up, he heard her calling him:

"Hey!"

He didn't answer. All he wanted was for her to go, for her to leave him alone, for her to quit going around asking stupid questions about prices and paint colors. At that time of day, the room was suffocating; the sun heated the roof like a grill and there were no windows to circulate the air. First he sweated from his forehead, then from his armpits and his hands. She can go to hell. Just leave me in peace. At the three-minute mark he heard her walk to the exit. Then he heard the car take off. People have less patience all the time, he said to himself. Yesterday's customer lasted seven minutes.

He left right after she did, waiting just long enough for her not to see him, then he locked the door after putting up the sign: BACK SOON.

He entered the Lontananza and ordered a beer. As he drank it, he observed the bartender with envy. Now, he really had a prosperous business, with customers at any time of day, and the freedom to sell whatever brands he wanted to sell. Besides, everyone who came through that door accepted any exchange without a fuss. "Give me a shot of Presidente." "I only have Viejo Verjel." "Okay, give me that." In the Lontananza it didn't matter if everything was white, black, or blue. And that wasn't all, the customers didn't argue about the price or carefully read the ads in the newspaper. This was indeed a noble business. Why the hell, Rubén asked himself, did I put up a paint store and not a bar?

He called the bartender over. Because of the empty bottles he bought for paint thinner, Rubén knew that at the Lontananza they served three brands of tequila: Sauza, Herradura, and Cuervo.

"Bring me a bottle of Orendain," he said.

"We don't have it," said the bartender, "but if you want, I can bring you—"

"Orendain or nothing," Rubén interrupted.

They stared at each other for a few moments. Rubén could tell how angry the bartender was when he responded:

"Nothing."

Then he smiled and left satisfied, feeling justified in not paying for the beer. The bartender made no move to go after him.

Rubén went back to his shop. Before he could get in he heard the phone ringing again. He didn't hurry to open the door; he wanted to see if his wife would let it ring more than fourteen times. But it suddenly occurred to him that it might not be Clara, and he ran to pick up. All he heard was the dial tone, and without hesitating he took advantage of being right there to call home.

"Clara."

"Yes, Rube."

"Why did you call me?"

"I told you, bad news, but I'll wait for you to get home."

"Yes," said Rubén, "that was the first time."

"The only time," she said.

There was a long silence. He hung up without saying good-bye. He was thinking about a long four-lane highway crossing the whole country from north to south, needing not only the center line, but lines on each side, six lines in all.

"Mundo!" he cried. "Why didn't you answer it?"

By the lengthening shadows he figured it was past noon. All he could do was wait the rest of the afternoon for that person, whoever it might be, to call again.

He tried to relieve the boredom by various means. He tried taking a siesta, but the heat kept him awake. He bought the afternoon paper and read it from start to finish, including the TV guide and the interesting classified ads. He tried solving the crossword puzzle on the next-to-last page, but he was defeated by number seven across: *A musical instrument made from a gourd with little stones inside.* He checked the filled-in crossword at the bottom of the page, but it turned out to be the solution to the one from the day before.

"I'd have to be nuts to buy this paper again."

He went out on the street to play biographies. He and Mundo would resort to this game every day to fight off the boredom.

An obese woman passed by. She was about forty and wore a sleeveless blouse out of which tumbled two enormous arms. On the left one you could see, like a bright, whitish stamp, the scar of an old vaccination. She constantly pushed her skirt down because every few steps it would crawl up over her knees.

She's been just as fat since childhood, Rubén thought. Only at the time she harbored dreams of being a singer. Her mother made her sing at family gatherings, to the disgust of her uncles and aunts. Of course, she never developed a voice to match her dreams, and with that body, who would ever dare put her on television?

Rubén canceled his thoughts at one stroke. He felt they were too plain and lacked originality. The failure of others was of no use to him without someone with whom to share it. If Mundo had been there, they would have developed her whole life: some reason that would have prevented her from ever being happy; her marriage to a sick, penniless old man who sought, not a woman's companionship, but a nurse's care; her habit of singing everything she heard on the radio, even the jingles; her frustration when her husband died so soon there was no time to conceive a child.

He lost sight of the woman when she turned a corner. It's no fun to play biographies alone, he thought, and as he entered his shop again, he thought that maybe it had never been fun, but with Mundo at least there had been a way to fool himself by pretending to laugh.

The streetlights came on and the cars began cruising by with their headlights on. Rubén realized it was time to leave, to return home to get the bad news his wife had ready for him. BACK SOON, he read, and he asked himself if he would have the stomach to return the next day.

He left the place slowly, his ears alert just in case there was a last ring of the telephone. He crossed the street and decided to sit on the curb for a while, to observe his business from there. He saw the sheet-metal sign that read *The Big Brush,* under a great big brush painting a rainbow, the plate-glass windows multiplying the Cope Paints logo, and the red awning from which hung the catch phrase HIGHER QUALITY AT A LOWER PRICE. A taxi stopped in front of him, blocking his view. The driver revved his motor various times in neutral, casting him an obliging glance.

"I don't need a ride," said Rubén, and he set off on foot.

He had gone two blocks when he heard voices coming from a house. It was two women, apparently mother and daughter, because one was scolding the other for the bad grades she had received and threatened her with not letting her watch soap operas any more. The other excused herself by claiming her teachers had it in for her and the soaps had nothing to do with her grades. Rubén hesitated for a moment before knocking on the door.

The discussion quieted immediately. Just the same, a long while passed before they opened the door to him. First a light went on over the door, then the hinges creaked.

"Yes?" a girl barely fifteen peeked out.

"Pardon me," said Rubén, "do you carry Berel paint?"

The girl did not have the slightest idea what to answer. She just stared at the man standing before her with incredulous eyes. Then the door opened wider and revealed the figure of an ill-tempered woman.

"What do you want?" she asked.

"He wants to know if we carry Berel Paint ," said the girl.

The woman raised her voice, with a tone even more bitter than when she was prohibiting the soap operas.

"Get out of here, or I'll call my husband."

From the sense of alarm in the woman, Rubén understood that it was only a threat, that the husband, if he existed, was far away.

"I'm leaving because I want to," said Rubén. "Because you don't carry Berel."

He walked to the next block and again stood in front of a house. This time he chose it, not because of any yelling he heard inside, but because of the leprous look of the exterior. The pink paint had turned into a dust that blew off with each gust of wind and rain, letting the gray lattice show through. Rubén rubbed his hand over the wall and then tasted his fingers smeared with the pink dust. There was no doubt, it was Cope, the color called Charm Pink in the sampler. They had all been baptized with names that at the moment seemed absurd to him: Enchanting Blue, Oyster White, European Gray, Hope Green and Dreamy Green, Walnut Brown and Earth Brown.

He knocked a few times without anyone answering. Certain there was no one home, he started kicking the screen door. Just then he noticed that the lady with the vaccination scar was across the street. The singer, he thought.

"Sing something for me," he whispered. He would have preferred to yell it out, but he was out of breath from the kicking.

The woman realized that Rubén had talked to her and stopped.

"I couldn't hear you," she said.

Her voice turned out to be sweeter than Rubén could have imagined. It occurred to him that the woman was on her way home, where she would find a loving husband and two or three children who would kiss her on the cheek. She probably had never wanted to be a singer and never desired anything beyond her possibilities. He watched her cross the street and approach him.

"What can I do for you, mister?" she asked. "Do you need something?"

So amiable, so sweet, so close she became bothersome, to the point that Rubén could not stand her presence. He ignored her, turned around to knock on the door again and kept his back to her until he was sure she was gone. It mattered little to him that they had not answered. Anyway, he was still several blocks from home, and there were quite a few doors left to knock on. Besides, he would make a stop at the Lontananza. Nothing would please him more than spending the last of his money on a drink that would give him the patience to face up to Clara's bad news, to the telephone that didn't ring, to the twelve-color sampler, to the Dallas Cowboys T-shirt with number eighty on it, to sweet-voiced women. What did he care if they served him Orendain or Sauza or whatever. Now, what really mattered was that he get the most for his money, HIGHER QUANTITY AT A LOWER PRICE. Bring me whatever, the cheapest, even if it's as low-class as Cope Paints, even if afterward I have to pay for the empty bottle to fill it with thinner and plug it with a wad of rolled-up paper with a half-finished crossword puzzle on it.

Rubén looked up the street and saw the red taillights of a car fading away, and asked himself if perhaps maracas could be musical instruments made of gourds with little stones inside.

COYOTE
Juan Villoro

HILDA'S FRIEND, ALFREDO, HAD TAKEN THE BULLET TRAIN BEFORE BUT NOW HE enthused about the pleasures of a slow journey: they would cross the desert at a leisurely pace; as the hours went by, the horizon would no longer be in the windows but on their faces, reddened reflections of the earth upon which the peyote grew. To Pedro, Alfredo had seemed like an idiot; unfortunately, he only became certain of it after following his advice.

They changed trains in a village from which the rails stretched on to the end of the world. A wooden coach with too many live birds. The smell of animal droppings prevailed until someone urinated in the back somewhere. The benches were crammed with women whose youth had been punished by the dust, with neutral eyes that no longer hoped for anything. You would think they had rounded up a whole generation from the desert in order to carry them to an unknown extermination. A soldier dozed on his carbine. Julieta, trying to rescue something from that wretchedness, started babbling about magical realism. Pedro asked himself when it was that this imbecile had become a good friend.

Actually, the trip had begun to smell fishy when Hilda introduced Alfredo. People who dress entirely in black tend to either withdraw to the edges of monomania or to show off recklessly. Alfredo contradicted both extremes.

Everything about him eluded easy definitions: he wore a ponytail, he was a lawyer—international affairs: drug trafficking—, he consumed natural drugs.

With him, the group of six was complete: Clara and Pedro, Julieta and Sergio, Hilda and Alfredo. They had dinner at a place where the crepes seemed to be made of rubber. Sergio was highly critical of the flour; he was quite skilled at talking about such things. He announced that he would not take peyote; after a decade of psychotropic drugs—which included a friend throwing himself from the pyramid at Tepoztlán and four months in a hospital in San Diego—he was cured of temporary paradises:

"I'll keep you company, but I won't take anything."

No one was better suited than he to watch over them. Sergio was the kind of person who finds a use even for things he doesn't know how to use, and prepares exquisite stews with weird vegetables.

Julieta, his wife, wrote plays that, according to Pedro, enjoyed immoderate success: he treated every one of her works with scorn until it had played for the three-hundredth time.

Alfredo left the table for a moment (to pay the bill, making decisions for everyone in his quiet way) and Clara moved close to Hilda, said something in her ear; they laughed a lot.

Pedro looked at Clara, who was happy to be going to the valley with her best friend, and felt the intense, sad emotion of witnessing something good that was now irretrievable: Clara's glowing eyes no longer included him; tasting some of that old pleasure could end up hurting him. A memory wounded him with its remote happiness: Clara at the precise moment of her first encounter, open to the future and its promise, with her life still intact.

For weeks that seemed like months Pedro had railed against going back. Wasn't it a contradiction to repeat a rite of initiation? Did it make sense to seek the magic that they had ruined with two years of living together? Once, in another century, they had loved each other in the high desert. Where did the energy they had shared go? The naked fulfillment of those hours, perhaps the only hours during which they had existed with no consequences, with no other ties than themselves. Just this evening, in a city of numerous streets, they had argued over a broken umbrella. And it wasn't even the rainy season! What did her complaining, the cramped apartment, the broken appliances have to do with the forsaken paradise of the desert? No, there were no second trips. Just the same, seeing Clara's smile and her eyes like those of a child enchanted with the world, he realized that he would return. He had seldom desired her as much, although at that moment nothing would have been as difficult as being with her: Clara was somewhere else, beyond herself, on a trip that, in her own way, she had already begun.

The idea of taking a slow train won out with no opposition: pilgrims always chose the most arduous route. However, after only half a dog day, the choice seemed ill fated. It was then that Alfredo started talking about the bullet train. The look Pedro gave him reduced him to silence. Hilda bit her nails until she drew blood.

"Calm down, silly," Clara said to her.

At the next town Alfredo got off to buy juice: six oilcloth bags filled with some whitish water that everyone drank, just the same.

The earth slid by the windows, at times yellow, almost always red. In the evening they saw a broken skyline, the peaks that marked the entrance to the valley. They advanced so slowly that it was an added torture to see their destination appear suspended in the distance.

The train stopped at a wretched little store constructed of sheet metal in the middle of nowhere. Two men came aboard. They carried high-powered rifles.

After half an hour—which, compared to the length of the trip, seemed like a minute—they managed to make their way through the bodies seated in the aisle and settle down next to them.

Julieta had finished her juice; the soft bag lay warm in her hands. One of the men pointed to the liquid, and spoke to Sergio:

"Wouldn't you rather have something stronger, *compadre?*"

The canteen circulated from mouth to mouth. A burning mescal.

"You guys going deer hunting?" Sergio asked.

"Anything that moves," and pointed to the landscape, where nothing, absolutely nothing, moved.

The sun had affected the faces of the hunters in a strange way, as though burning them in patches: their cheeks ablaze from a circulation that did not reach the rest of their faces, their necks purplish. They had almost nothing to say but seemed quite anxious to say it; they fell all over each other talking to Sergio about hunting small game; they asked if they were going camping, their gaze all the while avoiding the women.

You only had to see Hilda's dark glasses to know they were going for peyote.

"The Huicholes don't travel by train. They walk all the way from the coast," the hunter's voice took on an aggressive edge.

Pedro wasn't the only one who saw Hilda's Walkman. Was there anything more ridiculous than those six spiritual tourists? They would surely get the worst end of that encounter on the train; nevertheless, as on so many improbable occasions, Julieta saved the situation. She blew her bangs out of her eyes and asked about the panners. One of the hunters took off his baseball cap and scratched his head.

"The people who dredge the river sand looking for gold," Julieta explained.

"There aren't any rivers around here," said the man.

The dialogue continued, just as absurdly. Julieta was working out a scene for her next play.

The hunters were going to a canyon called *"Sal si puedes."*

"Right over there," they remarked, the palms of their hands vertical, their five fingers pointing who knows where.

"Take a look," they offered the telescopic sight of one of the rifles: very far-away rocks, the air vibrating in the grooved circle.

"Are there any spotted deer left?" Sergio asked.

"Almost none."

"Pumas?"

"Naw!"

What animals justified the effort of going all the way to the canyon? A couple of jackrabbits, maybe a quail.

They said good-bye just as the sun began setting.

"Here. Just in case."

Pedro had not opened his mouth. He was so surprised at being chosen to receive the gift that he couldn't refuse. A hunting knife, with an inscription on the blade: *I belong to my owner.*

The sunset made up for the fatigue. A sky of intense blue that condensed into a final, red stripe.

The train stopped in a hollow surrounded by the night. Alfredo recognized the stop.

There wasn't even a corrugated tin roof for shelter in that place. They got off, feeling the painful relief of stretching their legs. A kerosene lamp waved from the engine as a signal that the train was leaving.

The night was so dense that you could only see three feet of rails in front of you. Just the same, they waited to light the lanterns: the sounds of insects, the hooting of an owl. The inert landscape they had observed all during the blazing day somehow revived them completely. In the distance, some sparks that could be fireflies. There was no moon, a sky full of fine grains of sparkling sand. They had done well after all: they were coming in through the right gate.

They lit the lamps. Alfredo led them to a depression where they found campfire ashes.

"The wind blows less here."

Only then did Pedro feel the insidious wind that blew through the round bushes.

"They call them 'witches,'" Sergio explained; then he started gathering rocks and branches. He lit a formidable bonfire that would have taken Pedro hours to make.

Clara suggested they look for constellations, knowing they would only find Orion's belt. Pedro kissed her; her fresh, wet tongue still had the burning taste of the mescal. They lay on the harsh ground and he thought he saw a shooting star.

"Did you see it?"

Clara had fallen asleep on his shoulder. He caressed her neck and the contact with her soft skin made him aware that he had sand on his fingers.

He awoke very early, his neck stiff as stone. The remains of the fire emitted the agreeable odor of burning wood. A clear blue sky, still without the sun.

A little later the six were drinking coffee, the only thing they would have that day. Pedro saw that their faces were content, although somewhat rank from the hassles of the trip, the hard, frozen night, the wall of prickly pear cactus where they went to urinate and defecate. Hilda looked like she had not slept in ages. She took out two aspirin tablets and drank them with her coffee.

"Stinking mescal," she said.

Alfredo rolled up his blanket with his boot and threw it over his shoulder, an archetypal move, right out of a cowboy commercial.

Pedro thought about the hunters. What were they looking for in that barren place? Alfredo seemed to guess what he was thinking because he started talking about caged animals being taken to zoos in other countries.

"They even take the roadrunners," he furiously brushed his hair, did up his ponytail. He pointed to an impressive cactus, "The Japanese uproot them and off they go, to the other side of the Pacific."

He had pending lawsuits concerning these things on his desk. Lawsuits on whose behalf? The owner of the desert? Some improbable guardian of that forest without water?

Pedro started walking. Clara's kiss had dried up immediately, a taste of dregs in his mouth. He breathed a clean, warm, insufferable air. Each one of them had to find his or her own peyote, the pale green buttons that hid from the unworthy. The idea that the desert was being ravaged churned in his mind.

He entered a field of mesquite and *huizaches*; in the background, a ridgeline served as a reference point to keep him oriented. "The desert air is so pure that things appear closer than they are." Who was it that had warned him about that? He advanced without getting close to the ridge. He fixed on a closer checkpoint: a tree that apparently had been split by lightning. The cacti made it impossible to walk in a straight line; he avoided a profusion of plants before arriving at the dead trunk full of red ants. He took off his straw hat as though the tree could still provide shade. His hair was soaking wet. At a short but incalculable distance the ridge rose, its flanks vibrating with a bluish tone. He took out his canteen, gulped a mouthful of water, and spat.

He kept walking, and after a while he perceived the beneficial effect of the sun: one could be cooked like that, infinitely, until bereft of all thought, without a word in one's head. A buzzard suspended in the sky, cactus fruit like bloodclots. The ridgeline was nothing more than an expanse that went from blue to green to maroon.

He felt more heat than exhaustion and he climbed without great effort, bathed in perspiration. At the top he looked at his wet ankles; his socks reminded him of televised tennis matches during which the commentators talked about dehydration. He lay down on a spot clear of thorns. His body exuded a sour odor, intense, sexual. For a moment he flashed upon a hotel room, a very poor tropical place where he had copulated with a nameless woman. The same smell of damp sheets, unfamiliar bodies, uncontrollable, the bed where a woman received him violently, fusing into a blaze that erased her features.

In what corner of the desert was Clara sweating? He did not have the energy to go on thinking. He stood up. The valley ran on, striped with shadows. An arduous immensity of wounded plants. The clouds floated, dense, sharply outlined, in a rigid, almost petrified formation. They did not block the sun; they only spread oily smudges on the high desert floor. Very far in the distance he saw some moving dots. They could be people. Huicholes following their *maracame*, perhaps. He was in the region of the five blue altars protected by the fabled deer. At night they would celebrate the rites of fire, where words are burned. What was the meaning of his being there, so far from the ceremony? Two years before, on a friend's ranch, they had drunk peyote shakes with a group of initiates. After the purgatory of nausea ("A drug for Mexicans!" Clara had complained), they exuded a thick, vegetable odor. Then, when they were convinced that the whole thing was nothing but suffering and vomit, came some mind-blowing hours: a pristine, cerebral electricity: asterisks, spirals, pink, yellow, celestial blue stars. Pedro went out to urinate and observed the solitary little town in the distance with its fluorescent walls. The stars were liquid and the trees palpitated. He broke a tree branch with his hands and felt endowed with explicit power. Clara was waiting for him inside, and for the first time he understood that he did protect her, in a physical way, against the cold and the unending earth; life acquired a proximity like one's blood, the countryside gave off a fresh smell, crazy, the light was reflected in the eyes of a girl.

Did it all have something to do with those nights of his life: her body burning in his hands in an almost forgotten port, Clara's eyes in front of the fireplace? And at the same time, did it have something to do with the city that beat them down bit by bit with its heavy responsibilities, its fractured schedules, its useless automation? Clara only knew of one solution for unhappiness: returning to the valley. Now they were there, surrounded by earth, their spirits somewhat vanquished by exhaustion, the sun that now and then managed to tear thoughts out of them.

In the distance the procession moved on, followed by a curtain of dust.

Pedro turned around: at an almost inconceivable distance he saw some colored spots that were probably his friends. He decided to move on; the ridgeline would serve to orient him, he would go back after a few hours to share his trip with the others. Just the same, for the time being, he could enjoy this vastness without roads, populated by cacti and minerals, open to the wind, to the clouds that would never cover it completely.

He climbed down the ridge and entered a forest of huizaches. All of a sudden he lost his perspective. It closed in on him totally: little birds jumped from nopal leaf to nopal leaf; purple cactus fruit, yellow ones. He imagined the place through which the Huicholes were moving, he imagined a direct route over the plants, and he tried to correct his broken steps. The task of avoiding the *magueyes* was so absorbing that he almost forgot the peyote; at some point he touched the oilcloth bag he wore on his belt, a burning rag, bothersome.

He arrived at an area where the ground took on a sandy consistency; the cacti parted, forming a clearing presided over by a great stone. A hexagonal block, polished by the wind. Pedro moved close: the rock was chest-high.

Odd that there were no ashes to be found, no crumbs, no vegetable paint, no evidence that others had experienced the attraction of the stone. He scraped his forearms climbing up. He studied the surface carefully. He knew nothing about minerals but he felt that a kind of ideal abstract perfection was consummated here. In some way the block established order in the dispersion of cacti, as though another kind of logic, plain, inextricable, were crystallized there. Those sharp edges were the farthest thing from a refuge: the stone served no purpose, but its brute simplicity was fascinating, like a symbol of the uses to which it could be put: a table, an altar, a cenotaph.

He stretched out on the stone hexagon. The sun had climbed very high. He felt his mind harden, almost inert. Even with his hat over his face and his eyes closed, he saw a vibrating, yellow movie. He feared sunstroke; he got up: the huizaches had iridescent circles around them. He looked in every direction. Only then did he realize that the ridge had disappeared.

At what point had the land taken him to that mesa? Pedro was unable to tell which side of the stone he had climbed. He looked for footprints left by his tennis shoes. Nothing. He could not make out any trail of dust thrown up by the pilgrims in the distance. His heartbeat quickened. He was lost in the immobile drift of that stone raft. He looked down, became dizzy at the idea of plunging into the green plants that flanked all sides. He searched for a sign, for anything that would reveal the path he had taken to the stone. A gray, artificial dot brought his sanity back. Right down there lay a button! It had come off his shirt as he climbed up. He jumped down and picked up the plastic circle, pleasant to the touch. After hours in the desert, he had made no discovery other than that part of his clothing. At least he knew from which direction he had come. Resolute, he walked toward the irregular, spiny horizon that was his way back.

Once again he tried to follow an imaginary straight line but he was forced to deviate. The vegetation got thick; there had to be an underground source of water in that region; the organ-pipe cactus rose way over his head, a chaos that opened and then closed in. He went forward sideways, ducking under the upraised arms of the organ-pipe cactus, ever mindful of the little clumps of cholla scattered over the ground.

He had strayed from his route: on his way in he had not passed through that tangle of hardened leaves. He was thinking only about getting out, of arriving at a paradise where there were less cacti, when he slipped and landed against a round plant, with its spines laid out in double file, which in a very precise, absurd manner, reminded him of a mock-up of a flu virus he had seen in a museum. The spines pierced his hands. Thick spines that he managed to pull out easily. He wiped the blood on his thighs. What the hell was he doing there, he, who when face-to-face with an unnamable plant, thought of a vinyl virus?

He took a long time looking for an aloe plant. When he finally found one, the blood had already dried on him. Just the same, he took out the hunting knife, cut a leaf and felt the healing properties of the sap on his wounds.

At some point he realized that he had not urinated all day. He found it difficult getting a few drops out; the perspiration was drying him up inside. He stopped to cut some cactus fruit. One of the few things he knew about the desert was that the skin of the prickly pear fruit had invisible spines. He cut up the fruit with his knife and ate greedily. Only then did he realize that he was dying of hunger and thirst.

From time to time he belched the perfumed aroma of the cactus fruit. The only pleasant thing in that endless solitude. The cacti forced him to take steps that could be tracing a single, imperceptible curve. The idea that he could be moving in an infinite circle made him scream, knowing full well that no one would hear him.

As the sun went down, he saw a jackrabbit leap, a covey of quail scurry by, fast animals that had avoided the heat. He noticed a bramble patch a few yards away and felt the desire to lie down among the sandy clumps of earth; only a demented person dared disturb the hours that made up the real desert night, its burning repose.

Then he kicked a pebble, then another; the earth became drier, a harsh sound under his shoes. He managed to walk a few yards without having to avoid the plants, a space that in that elemental moment was as good as a way out. He fell to his knees, exhausted, feeling a joy that in some humble, primal way, was related to the fact that the cacti were separating more and more.

When he started walking again, the sun was setting in the distance. A green swath appeared before his eyes. Surely an illusion created by his calcified mind. He supposed it would disappear sooner or later. The green belt remained. A palisade of prickly pear cactus, a definite, planted row, a fence. He ran to see what was on the other side: a desert identical to the one that extended, inexhaustible, behind him. The wall seemed to separate an image from its own reflection. He sat on a rock. He looked at the other desert again, with the resigned shock of someone contemplating a useless miracle.

He closed his eyes. The shadow of a bird caressed his body. He cried for a long time, surprised that his body could still shed that moisture.

When he opened his eyes the sun was taking on a deep tone. A watery star shone in the distance.

Then he heard a shot.

The knowledge that someone close by was killing something created an unexpected, animal joy in him. He yelled, or rather, he tried to yell: a soundless growl, as though his throat were full of dust.

Another shot. Then a challenging silence. He crawled toward the place from which the shots were coming: the good fortune of finding someone was beginning to blend with the fear of becoming someone's target. Perhaps he was not following a shot but its fleeting echo in the desert. Could he trust any of his senses? In spite of that, he kept on crawling, scraping his knees, his forearms, fearing an ambush, or even worse, arriving too late, when all that was left would be a trace of blood.

Pedro found himself in a place of low bushes, silent.

He raised himself into a crouching position: at a distance that seemed rather close, he could make out a circle of black birds. He walked upright again.

He reached an extremely arid area, a sea of limestone and fossils; from time to time, a thorn bush raised a bloodless stump. The circle of birds dissolved in a sky in which it was now difficult to make out anything but the stars.

His situation was so absurd that any change would make it better; he was as pleased at seeing the shadow of some huizaches as he had been before at escaping from the labyrinth of those plants.

He moved toward the curtain of shadows, and in the dark he disregarded the cactus leaves scattered on the ground. A prickly pear leaf nailed itself to his foot like a second sole. He pried it off with a knife, his eyes brimming with tears.

After a while he was surprised at how well he could walk with a wounded foot; fatigue was dulling his senses. He reached the bristling branches of the huizaches and had no time to catch his breath. On the other side, in a ravine, there were lamps, bonfires, intense activity. He thought it was the Huicholes performing their rites of fire; by some complicated trick of fate, he had reached the pilgrims. Just then, an immense shadow loomed over the desert. Something made an acid, creaking sound. Pedro discovered the crane, the tense block and tackle was raising a monstrous shape, a plant with many extremities that in the night appeared to be deranged tentacles. The men down there were uprooting an organ cactus. Pedro did not shudder; in the chaos of that day it was a minor disorder to confuse the Huicholes with the plant pirates. He braced himself to go down toward the excavation. There were cries in the camp, the cactus swayed in the air, the men kicked dirt on the fires, there were agitated shadows everywhere.

Pedro hit the dirt, landing on a vegetal, pestiferous substance. Another shot froze him in that putrefaction. The camp was returning fire. From some corner of his mind he heard the expression "crossfire," and there he was, in the line of fire at the point where the attackers become confused with the defenders. He prayed on that dark hill of sand, knowing that after the shoot-out he could not risk revealing himself to either band.

Afterward, as he was again walking toward an uncertain destination, he asked himself if he was actually moving away from the bullets or if he was about to fall into another deafening skirmish.

He stretched out on the ground but did not close his eyes, his eyelids stiff from a tense exhaustion; he also realized, with infinite sadness, that closing his mind's eyes now provided his only chance for getting back: he did not want to imagine Clara's soft hands, nor the light around which his friends were talking about him; he could not give in to that madness in which his return became a precise image in his mind.

He had become accustomed to the dark; nevertheless, rather than actually seeing it, he felt something strange closing in on him. A warm body had entered the darkness. He turned around, very slowly, trying to control his surprise, nearly fracturing his neck bones, his blood pumping in his throat.

Nothing could have prepared him for the encounter: a three-legged coyote stared at Pedro, his fangs bared, his jaws issuing a steady growl, almost purring. Pedro could see the animal was bleeding. He could not take his eyes off the bloody stump; he moved his hand toward his knife and the coyote leapt upon him. Its jaws clamped on his fingers; he managed to protect himself with his left hand while his right hand struggled to get past the wild kicking. With his knife, he stabbed and slashed open the three-legged animal. He felt its chest bathed in blood, its fangs relaxed their hold. The last contact: its tongue softly licking his neck.

A singular energy possessed his limbs: he had survived, hand-to-hand. He wiped the blade of his knife and cut up his shirt to cover his wounds. The animal lay there, enormous, on a black stain. He tried to carry it, but it was too heavy. He knelt, extracted the hot viscera and felt an inexpressible relief at sinking his wounded hands into that hot, wet mass. His struggle with the coyote had taken seconds; it took hours to struggle with its carcass. He finally managed to get its pelt off. He could not be too sure of what would happen, but he threw it over his back, proudly, and started walking again.

Exultation does not repeat its moment; Pedro could not describe his sensations, he moved on, still full of that instant, his body alive, breathing the acrid wind loaded with fine particles of metal.

He looked at the starry sky. Somewhere else Clara was also looking at a sky unknown to them.

From time to time he was hurt by spiny branches. He was at the end of his physical capacity. Something stuck in his thigh, he pulled it out without stopping. At some moment he became aware that he was carrying an unsheathed knife. It was very difficult to get it back in its sheath; he was losing control of the least of his motor functions. He fell to the ground. Before or after he fell asleep he looked at the starry vault, radiant sand.

He awoke with the coyote's pelt stuck to his back, wrapped in an acrid smell. It was dawn. He felt a saline taste in his mouth. He heard a very close buzzing; he stood, surrounded by flies. The desert vibrated like a diffuse space. He had trouble focusing on the promontory in the distance and this perhaps mitigated his happiness: he had returned to the ridge.

He reached the down slope at midday. The burning sun beat down vertically, his temples pulsated, fevered; in spite of that, he was able to make out a clear landscape: the other valley and two columns of smoke. The campground.

He walked straight toward the distance where his friends were, at a pace that seemed fast to him but was surely extremely slow. He arrived as evening fell.

After getting lost in a land where all was green followed by brown, he felt an incommunicable joy at seeing colored shirts. He called out, or at least he tried to call out. A dry hiss made Julieta turn around and let out a real howl.

He didn't move until he heard steps approaching with unheard-of energy: Sergio, the protector, with a look of bothered lucidity on his face, and a gaze of intense reproach, and Clara, her face pale, awake all night from having waited up for him.

Sergio stayed back a few yards, perhaps so that Clara would be the first to embrace him. Pedro closed his eyes, anticipating the hands that would surround him. When he opened them, Clara was still there, three very long steps away.

"What have you done?" she asked, in a tone of tired surprise, very much like disgust.

Pedro gulped thick saliva.

"What is that shit?" Clara pointed to the pelt on his back.

He remembered the nocturnal combat and attempted to communicate his dark victory. He had saved himself! He brought a trophy! But all he could do was make a confused gesture.

"Where were you?" Sergio took a step toward him.

Where? Where? Where? The question reverberated in his head. Where were the others, in what corner were they hallucinating that scene? Pedro fell to his knees.

"What a fucking mess! Why?" Clara's voice was taking on an abrasive tone.

"Give me the canteen," Sergio ordered.

He took a cold gulp and drank the liquid that ran down his face, a bitter taste, in which his blood and the animal's were mixed.

"Let's get that fucking thing off you," proposed an obsessive voice, capable of saying "fucking thing" with infinite calm.

He felt as if they were taking a scab off him. The pelt dropped next to his knees.

"What a stink, damn!"

There was a slow silence. Clara knelt next to him, without touching him; she looked at him from an indefinable distance.

After a while, Sergio returned with a shovel:

"Bury it, bro," and touched him on the neck, his first contact after the battle with the coyote, a touch with electrifying softness. "He needs to be left alone."

They walked away.

It was getting dark. He touched the pelt with which he had trekked across the desert. He smiled and a sharp pain pierced his cheeks; any useless gesture had become a waste of life. He raised his eyes. The sky was again filling with unknown stars. He started digging.

He threw the mess into the hole and patted the earth carefully, forming a soft mound with his sore hands. He propped his neck on the sand. Just before he fell asleep he heard a sob, but he didn't try to open his eyes. He had come back. He could sleep. Here. Now.

WHY COME BACK?
(PLAYING WITH FIRE)
Mónica Lavín

WHEN A WOMAN LEAVES, YOU SHOULD NOT LET HER COME BACK HOME. BUT how was I to ignore her; she stood outside the door all night. She knocked and I asked who it was. Go away I said. She didn't say another word. I heard the wool of her coat rubbing against the wood as she slid down and sat on the step. I imagined her hugging the handbag she took when she left. The large weekend bag, the one we used when, every once in a long while, we would get it into our heads to leave the city. I dropped the eggs into the frying pan and the sizzling of the oil almost certainly covered the sound she made as she blew her nose. It was November; in this part of the city it's always cold at night and the cold makes her nose run. I took the eggs out and put them on a plate with a slice of ham. It was the last slice; since she left I buy very little. I had never done the shopping before. At first I would buy by the pound, but when after a week I had to throw out a slimy green mess of sausage, I realized that half a pound was enough. I was beginning to enjoy going to the supermarket. It was a clean, well-lit place. At home I only turned on the light in the TV room and the bedroom. I never turned on the little entry light where Marta was now squatting in the dark.

I attacked the yokes with a hunk of bread. I buried my eyes in the yellow magma that slipped about on the coagulated egg white. Hearing her breathing irritated me. We shouldn't have bought this cheaply made house; you can hear everything. When we moved in we could hear the neighbors flush their toilet, and, along with our last unmarried son, we would play at guessing who it was. Marta used to laugh. Back then, with Julian at home, she used to laugh a lot. He pampered her, and she him. Girls, it would have been better to have a girl to spoil me. I always suspected that the bastard she left with was like Julian, always smiling, endearing. But flattery and long embraces are not for me. A look that digs deep is enough, like when I said good-bye to Marta as she put on her brown coat.

"You won't try to stop me?" she asked, her feelings hurt.

"You want to go. There's nothing I can do."

"Maybe you think it's paradise here by your side?"

"It's just here by my side."

Why was she outside the door now? Three months apart were not enough to suture one's soul; the pain kept on gushing like the egg yokes I was so hurriedly devouring to hush the certainty of her return with my jaws.

If she wants to be a bitch, let her sleep like a bitch, I thought, downing the beer I drank every night to help me sleep. It was painful not falling into the melodrama, not admitting how difficult it was to sleep without Marta's body by my side, without her smell of creams and wilted woman. I felt the cynical desire to bid her goodnight as I dragged my slippered feet upstairs.

Wasn't she in love when she left? Wasn't she honest enough to hurt me with the truth? *You need a man at your side, don't you? You can't make it on your own.* I couldn't make it on my own either. That's what made me furious. I hated her being away; I hated her for humiliating herself by being outside the door, and I hated her for wanting to be by my side again. She had deceived me. No, not when she left. Even in my misery, I admired that she could change, that she could say it's everyone for himself. Maybe life could be more cordial. But she had once again chosen this shared death, because habit is comforting and annihilating and mutual understandings fill in the silences. You find yourself making payments on a mortgaged destiny.

The bed feels cold, frozen; that's how beds always are when we violate them. And it's unmade, full of crumbs, without the courtesy Marta paid the sheets so they would accept the calm of our sleep. The bed was enemy territory. My life had become enemy territory. At first I felt enough rage to try to find her and come to blows with my rival. But she had left, what sense did it make to beat up the man who offered her another temporary station? Perhaps that's what love was, station platforms on a long voyage. There are those who never leave the station. Something is always missing from their suitcases. Marta left so sad that she forgot her suitcase. Not graceful, completely undone. She couldn't get angry with me, she never could, not even when I kept quiet and she talked about Julian and his jazz lessons.

Why come back? Did she add things up? Did the suitor prove unsuitable? Does he have bad breath, or wake up in a bad mood? She has come back to grow old with me. To discuss the silence of being in her sixties, the epilogue of thirty-five years of marriage. Let her die from the cold; let her blow her nose all night; may the snot become stalactites in her red nose.

Once again fried eggs for breakfast, the news on television. I think she's left, or maybe she died from the cold. Maybe we're both dying from the cold. Marta always yelled, *Your sweater, Victor, don't forget to put on your sweater!* I wasn't a child. I would put it on grumbling. Wives become mothers; husbands become children. Julian and I never got along well. One day he told me he was inviting his mother out for supper. You don't like to go out at night, Pop.

They came back laughing, reeking of wine. I didn't talk to them the next day. *You have bad breath,* I said to them. Surely Marta over there behind the door has that overnight bad breath. The yellow lava spread over the egg white again and I trapped it violently with the stale bread. Then I heard her move. She heard my slippers shuffling and got the courage to call out to me, *Victor, please.*

There are bitches that live inside the house, I thought, and I opened the door as she leaned against it. She lost her balance and fell on the floor, halfway into the house. Without looking at her, I went back to the table. Gracias, Victor, she said as she fixed her hair, and standing there, still carrying her bag and hugging her coat, she shook off the cold of the night.

At first her steps were tentative; she asked permission to make herself breakfast, to shower, to watch television with me, to call Julian. And the dark shadows under her eyes and the fear and docility wore off, until she was once again the lady of her house, as she had always been. Only every once in a while would I notice her flaccid arms and imagine them around another body and then I detested her. I would hear her laugh at something on television and her joy would remind me of the bed, unmade for three months, and her laughter somewhere else. We never spoke about our situation. The usual silence and the silence of habit ended up putting the pieces in place.

We seldom looked each other in the face, and had never made love again. Marta didn't dare oppose my punishment, and I didn't want to stir up my rancor. One morning, at breakfast, as I looked at the sunny yoke on my plate, Marta extended a loving hand and touched my forearm. I need your caresses, Victor. That was all she had to say to make me grip my fork and nail that hand that had brushed against me to the table.

Now the silence is total; she fondles her ruined hand as we have breakfast, as we watch television, as we sleep, as she absently looks at the door I opened for her one day.

GINSBERG'S TIE
Juvenal Acosta

for Ma Jean and Chuck Triebel

I could hear the human noise we sat there making,
not one of us moving, not even when the room went dark.
—Raymond Carver

THE TWO COUPLES HAD GOTTEN TOGETHER TO HAVE A FEW MARTINIS AND then go somewhere to eat. The martini thing had made a comeback lately, a civilized custom common in a city that fancied itself as excessively civilized and extolled itself as not at all common. Still, Berkeley in the late nineties was no longer what it had been three decades before, in spite of what its inhabitants might think. The 1968 mirror in which the people of Berkeley foolishly saw themselves had been distorted by thirty implacable years during which its citizens, some of them ex-radicals of that decade, had accumulated dollars in their bank accounts and pounds around their bellies and hips.

Kevin returned to the living room with Don's second martini.

"It's really ironic that after all these years our drinks are the same as our parents'," Kevin said, attempting to reanimate the conversation which, after meandering about the arid lands of local politics without much conviction, threatened to abort the evening at any moment.

In the living room, decorated with all the exotic flare of expensive San Francisco import stores, Susan and Clare occupied the sofa near the fireplace and Don sat in a black leather armchair.

"And not only the drinks, the music too, and now even the clothes. Have you seen the kids in the Mission District dressing in this retro style?" Don said. "But

97

that's just what it's about. You're born, grow up, leave home running from your parents, only to find yourself after all those years doing everything possible to be just like them. That seems to be the rule although no one admits it. And if you have children," he went on as he sat up to reach for the martini Kevin offered him, "it's just a matter of time before they do the exact same thing."

Kevin and Don were not actually ex-radical leftists. Like the majority of their generation, they had both experienced their share of marijuana and tepid rebellion. Like many of their generation, Kevin and Don had gone through the sixties, and then the seventies, trying to sleep with as many girls as possible. Finally, like so many others of their generation, they both ended up breathing a deep sigh one day, and going to the barbershop to get their hair cut, and after a few years, on a given Sunday, they found themselves wearing Bermuda shorts and Birkenstocks in the middle of a shopping center, carefully considering the problem of which was a better investment, one Armani suit or two by Calvin Klein. Kevin and Don had concluded that they had to be practical, that the world did not need either one of them in particular for any specific project, that they must take care of themselves first, and then, if there was any time left, they could dedicate themselves to some humanitarian cause. Meanwhile, they would go on voting for the Democratic Party and donating annually to some politically correct charitable institution.

Susan looked at Clare and they both sighed in recognition that what was taking place before them was a familiar scene.

"Here we go with the middle-age crisis again," said Susan. "Why don't you resign yourself to accepting the fact that deep inside you both want to be exactly like your fathers and for both of us to be the spitting images of your mothers? Why not accept it once and for all, just to spare us this dialogue every time we get together?"

Susan stretched her body cat-like on the sofa. Clare gazed at her and, smiling in complicity, raised her eyebrows and lifted her glass of Sonoma merlot to her lips. The two women were just over forty, shared the status of second wives to their husbands, tried to meet at the gym, and occasionally went shopping together at the Walnut Creek mall. They were not close friends, but being the wives of husbands who were close friends brought them together in a relationship they both found comfortable.

*

Clare's eyes were like her name. Deep inside there was something strangely inexpressive. Don used to say that she had always been somewhat "peculiar," and he loved euphemisms as much as he loved his wife. Clare appeared eternally absent and only those who knew her a bit knew how to avoid that uncomfortable sensation her silence created. In spite of this, they were a pleasant couple; Don's open, extroverted character served as a counterbalance to Clare's "peculiar," eccentric serenity.

Kevin, for his part, loved Susan less than he had loved his first wife. He frequently thought about the fact that theirs was an investment partnership, a business owned by two people whose common objective was a comfortable, quiet old-age in some little town in New Mexico or Arizona. Susan was a successful, ambitious, tough real-estate agent. Kevin had married her because she was the opposite of his first wife. There were two types of pacts between them: contractual ones and those that had never been mentioned overtly. They frequently slept in separate bedrooms. They frequently drank more than two drinks over their limit to be able to have sex without inhibitions. Theirs was a relationship of mutual respect, of previously established limits such as the premarital agreement their respective lawyers had drawn up, their separate investment portfolios, and even Kevin's silence when she came home late and he suspected that it wasn't the sale of a house that was responsible for the happiness reflected on her face.

Clare got up to go to the bathroom and stopped in midstride.

"May I ask a question?"

The three turned to look at her inquisitively.

"When I pee," she said looking directly at Kevin, "can you hear me through the wall?"

They stared at her, surprised. Don cleared his throat and peeked at Kevin out of the corner of his eye, but didn't say a word. Kevin shrugged and arched his eyebrows, not knowing what to do, and Susan said that if she would rather use one of the two bathrooms on the second floor, she should.

Clare did not respond and went toward the bathroom on the lower floor. Susan got up and walked toward the kitchen.

Kevin and Don couldn't manage to fill the void produced by the silence of the situation. Each pretended to occupy his thoughts with different things. But both knew where their thoughts were.

The noise of Clare's pee hitting the water in the toilet began to filter through the wall; at first it was a timid, crystalline sound, that, as the now-long seconds it took to empty her kidneys transpired, grew, and invaded the living room in which no one spoke. Her unheard-of question had endowed her urinary waste with an extraordinary leading role. The act of getting up to urinate, which could have and should have gone by completely unnoticed, dominated the seconds it took within that now not-so-private space.

While they listened to the powerful stream of Clare's urine, Don and Kevin avoided looking at each other. The noise of her peeing was followed by a pause during which both were forced to imagine that Clare was now probably wiping her vaginal lips with a piece of toilet paper. Moments later the sound of the toilet flushing reached them, the toilet that would move that yellowish water through its pipes to the city's underground drainage system. Her urine would quickly cover the distance that would take it from the Berkeley Hills to the torrent of organic waste that would then be processed in a sophisticated treatment plant before being transported to the sea. Clare came out of the bathroom and once again sat in the living room chair. In silence, both men avoided her gray eyes. Kevin longed for his smoking days; he couldn't figure out what to do with his hands.

*

"This place is like a funeral parlor; turn on some music," Susan ordered as she returned from the kitchen with a plate of Brie cheese and bran crackers.

Kevin got up to look for a CD in his spacious office and returned in a few moments. *Old Blue Eyes getting a kick out of you.*

"What's the matter?" Susan asked, searching in their three faces for an explanation for the silence that had suddenly invaded the living room.

Don assured her nothing was wrong and then tried putting the conversation back on its original course.

"Remember the time we went to that reading by Allen Ginsberg in San Francisco? It was probably a couple of years ago, a few months before he died. Remember the comment one of you women made because he was wearing a tie? I think you mentioned an ideological contradiction or something like that. You remember?"

Kevin was spaced out, his gaze lost in the contemplation of some corner that wasn't in his house. Susan said that it was she who had asked how it was possible that a Beat poet, a hero of transgression and of all the rebels of all those decades, could dare put on an Establishment uniform; the tie was, after all, a powerful symbol of conformity with the System.

Clare and Kevin were still somewhere else. Since Clare was a quiet person, it didn't seem strange that when the four of them got together, she would isolate herself in an inoffensive silence. Usually Clare's silence was not apathetic, but respectful, clearly inquisitive, the silence of someone honestly interested in the discussion, someone who has chosen to keep quiet in order to better absorb what is being said. But that night something had happened, and her silence revealed that her mind was not there, that she had withdrawn from the conversation.

They went on drinking.

"I think we'd best kill that bottle of vodka before we go. You get to drive tonight, dear," said Kevin getting up from his armchair and carrying Don's and his glasses to the kitchen.

"Anything you say, sir," said Susan; she shrugged and smiled as she watched Don make a funny gesture of resignation with his eyebrows and his hands.

Kevin and Don had met one summer many years before while working construction to help cover their school expenses. They were both students at UC Berkeley and neither had any experience in construction. The regular working guys played pranks on them all day long, not only because of their rich-boy looks, but also because they were students, but after a few weeks, they accepted them as buddies. On Fridays they would go get drunk together

101

at Brennan's, an old Irish bar frequented by construction workers and intellectuals with a democratic bent. When classes resumed in September, they continued to get together on their own account. Kevin graduated as a lawyer and Don as an architect. They lost touch with each other for a few years because Don went off to Italy to do graduate work, married a girl from New York in Florence, and didn't return until after the marriage had quietly failed. Kevin had found work in a San Francisco law firm that made him a partner after a few years and he never left the Bay Area. He'd married young, a Peruvian girl who for two years cuckolded him with every black male she could find until one day he met Susan, who provided him with the strength and support he needed to get out of his marriage in a more or less dignified manner. The two friends found each other again when Don returned to Berkeley. Over the years, they both made money. They drove expensive cars, played Sunday tennis on the courts at the Montclair Hotel, and went out to dine as couples. This was only one more of their joint evening ventures.

*

"You remember Fatso Martinez?" asked Don.

Kevin looked at him as though the question had been asked in a foreign language.

"Martinez?"

"Martinez. The foreman at the company where we worked the summer of '67, when we met . . . I ran into him two or three weeks ago, at a gas station."

"Really?" Kevin responded, trying to shake off his distracted feeling.

"Yeah. I was cleaning my windows and I saw him get out of a brand-new Cadillac. He's just the same. I think the truth is he didn't remember me. But he told me he owns a small chain of Chinese restaurants. He lives in Martinez. Fatso Martinez from Martinez, proprietor of Chinese restaurants. Interesting. That Fatso's rolling in dough."

"But we all made dough," said Kevin in a sarcastic tone.

Don suspected that Kevin's mental state had to do with Clare and he felt the friendly obligation to rescue him.

"Depends on what we call dough. You know how much money Bill Gates made this week? I think it was published Wednesday in the *New York Times* . . . Three billion dollars . . . Three billion . . . Three thousand million dollars. Son of a bitch. Compared to him, you and I are a couple of bums."

"I've never seen a bum driving a BMW," replied Kevin almost gruffly. He picked up his drink and downed it. "Besides, whatever that imbecile earns or doesn't earn in the middle of this stinking decade in which a guy like Gates, a geek, a faggot nerd, who fifteen years ago could maybe aspire to a moderately comfortable life as a CPA thanks to his talent with numbers, is now a real Master of the Universe, with the power to sit in his office and dictate the direction every economy, every institution should take . . . you know what bugs me the most about Gates? His false modesty, his humility in front of the cameras . . . I think it's a thousand times better to be someone who feels comfortable with what he has, who flaunts it, who shows it off. But that guy in his Macy's T-shirts, dressed like a bank clerk on a weekend . . .

Susan cut him off, somewhere between impertinent and curious.

"What's wrong with you, Kevin? You're yelling . . ."

Kevin looked at her incredulously, took off his glasses, and with his index finger and thumb rubbed the bridge of his nose where two reddish marks appeared on the spots where his glasses were propped.

"Sorry," he said, appearing confused, and he got up to pour himself another drink in the kitchen.

*

Don went out on the terrace and Susan followed him.

"I agree with you," Susan said, putting an arm around his shoulder.

"With me? In regard to . . . ?"

"In regard to whatever, dear . . ."

Don sighed deeply. His eyes tried to penetrate the dense fog that covered the bay. Behind that curtain lay San Francisco. It was Saturday. At that hour, the restaurants and clubs would be full of couples, the bars full of singles of all ages. The thought filled him with melancholy. At times he reproached himself for not ever having had the courage to fulfill his desire to live alone. He always missed the short time he had intensely lived his freedom. He had returned from Italy to discover that in his absence, California had turned into one big party. The memory of those two years when he had money, a car, an apartment to which he returned with a different girl every weekend, tortured him every time something from those times came back to his memory. Then he met Clare.

On nights such as this, for a few melancholic moments, Don would indulge the fantasy of leaving Clare to go live in San Francisco across the bay, for a life of double martinis in nightclubs and seductions that would demand absolutely nothing more of him than the shallow ease of uncommitted relationships.

*

From his armchair, Kevin watched his best friend and his wife embracing tenderly. The scene gave him a feeling of calm happiness. He felt fortunate. They must love each other. How could they not, they're the people I love the most.

"They make a beautiful couple," said Clare, almost reading his thoughts.

"Not only that, they make a better couple than she and I do."

"And you and I . . . what kind of couple would we make?" Clare asked, coming out of her isolated state.

"I'm not sure. Probably one like them. You know why people get married? I don't think we do it because destiny or life gives orders that we humans blindly obey. I don't believe that reality is so sophisticated or chance so exact that it can create perfect couples, with each person absolutely necessary to the other. I believe that people, an individual, we, marry because at a given moment you believe that the other person understands what you've barely begun to figure out, a question you've barely begun to ask. Then the other person seems to confirm that series of intuitions or suspicions and you convince yourself that he or she has found the answer. Or you think that the formulation of that question that you've barely begun to ask yourself is better articulated by the mouth of that stranger, be it man or woman. And add the flesh to all that. Add to that marvelous misunderstanding the flesh's answer, the prodigious answer of reciprocal desire. How could you not desire that deception, that absolutely necessary illusion? We get married by mistake. We are the result of indispensable misunderstandings."

Kevin looked at Clare and for the first time discovered she was beautiful. Clare's eyes had dissolved and two large tears rolled down her cheeks.

Clare got up, and without looking back at him, went to the bathroom again. To avoid hearing her piss, Kevin quickly went to the kitchen to pour himself another drink.

*

They were again seated around the fireplace.

"Why an ideological contradiction?" Clare asked.

They all turned to look at her, not understanding.

"What contradiction are you referring to?" asked Kevin.

"Ginsberg's tie . . ." Clare mumbled, as though embarrassed.

"No, my dear," said Susan, "It was an exaggeration on my part . . . something silly, something left over from my adolescence of those years. Look at us. I was going to be a writer. For years all I did was go to readings by depressed poets on Telegraph Avenue, looking for lovers who carried around cheap editions of Rimbaud as their credentials, mistreating anyone who didn't have the right clothes or the proper attitude for the spiritual revolution of which I was to be the high priestess. Berkeley things back in those days. Imagine how I felt when after many years I got to be the agent for the owner of the home on Milvia Street where Ginsberg began writing *Howl*. The same house where Kerouac spent short periods with him, writing his books, sleeping with girls like me, who were looking for someone who spoke to the gods, who dialogued with the angels of psychedelics, who entered the most far-out corners of the labyrinths of consciousness and unconsciousness. I had long forgotten those times. And when a few months ago I found out that the house I had to sell was the same one where Ginsberg had lived, I began buying up the biographies of all of them. In some book I found two or three photographs of the house as it was back then. Photos of Ginsberg embracing Kerouac, one of Neal Cassady sitting on the sidewalk in the front yard. For some probably stupid reason, it embarrassed me to be part of the system that put a price on that property. But I sold it in a few weeks and that transaction became my own tie, my own way of negotiating my adult life along with all the other things. The house, I told myself, was neither Ginsberg, nor *On the Road,* nor Jim Morrison, nor a rock hurled at one of Reagan's soldiers. The house was simply a building with two bedrooms, one shitty bathroom, leaks in the ceiling and a foundation infested with termites, like us, like our ideas after all these years. Time dissolves ideological contradictions. Time dissolves everything."

Clare didn't say anything. Kevin and Don kept silent. If they had been asked, none would have been able to answer precisely how long they remained there, staring at their vodkas without touching them. Nor could they have answered how much longer they would go on, sunk into the immobility of that betrayed city, in the midst of the years that had finally arrived with all their uncompromising weight. It was getting dark and it was some time since the CD had finished playing, making the living room float in the dense fog of that silence. Don only hoped his wife wouldn't want to go to the bathroom again.

THE HOSTAGE

Álvaro Uribe

to Víctor Herrera

HE HAD TO TOUCH HIS EYES TO MAKE SURE HE WASN'T BLINDFOLDED. CARE-fully, he felt the delicate flesh of his eyelids, and through them, the tautness of his eyeballs. The motion caused him no pain. He withdrew his hand and blinked a few more times, but everything stayed the same. He still felt a pressure around his head that was not quite painful. He could see absolutely nothing.

He placed a hand on the nape of his neck. Something cold, smooth, and hard was tied around his head, perhaps a metal band. He traced it with his fingers: it was flat, about two inches wide, followed the curvature of his bones, ran over his ears, and ended at his temples. A softer material protruded along its edges, maybe plastic or foam rubber that allowed the metal to be adjusted without doing him any harm. He tried to take off the uncomfortable object, but an intense pain stopped him. The stabbing pains diminished little by little, finally converging in the back of his head.

A pain in that part of his skull was the last thing he remembered before the darkness in which he was now lost. Cautiously, he touched the point from which the pangs originated. There was the metal band that, he supposed, was a kind of blindfold. A little lower, near his neck, his hair was matted. He thought it was a clot of his own blood, and thinking of the blood made him remember Jenkins.

His memory cleared. Before losing consciousness he had seen poor Jenkins, Jenkins, who had not even managed to get his car door open, laid spread-eagled over the trunk, facedown, his back soaked with blood. His blood poured out of two or three wounds, streamed down the splashguards and over the license plate of the Embassy of the United States. Next to Jenkins's body stood the two men who had stabbed him. Their faces, livid under the white light of the street lamps, could have been Turkish or Palestinian, Syrian or Iranian, Armenian or Kurdish; they could have been the faces of any of the countless enemies of Uncle Sam in the Near East. He would not have been able to identify them now. What he remembered best were the hands of the attackers, holding knives that threatened him. He had managed to say to them, in a cracked voice that sounded nothing like his own:

"I don't have anything to do with this, *rien a voir*. I'm Mexican, *mexicain*."

And then the pain in the back of his neck and the complete darkness he still could not escape.

He figured that along with the murderers there had been a third individual who stood behind him and delivered the knockout blow. Afterward, they had stuffed him in a car, brought him to this dark room, and locked him in. Painfully, he figured that his captors were probably members of one of the many terrorist organizations, or agents of one of the many governments who, in order to further one of their many just causes, had decided to make a hostage of a secretary of the Embassy of the United States in France. But that idiot Jenkins, emboldened either by the dinner wine or the military training of North American diplomats, had tried to defend himself. And he, who had nothing to do with this affair, had been the victim of an unfortunate coincidence, that of dining with Jenkins precisely on the night chosen for his kidnapping.

"You've made a mistake," he screamed in the dark. "*Vous vous trompez.*"

His screams reverberated in what was almost an echo, but never quite made it. The room probably had little furniture, or at least few upholstered objects to deaden the sounds. There were probably no windows, either, since his eyes, which had had enough time to become accustomed to the dark, could not perceive the slightest glimmer of light. He was sitting on the ground, with his shoulders against the wall. He felt around and ascertained that there was no rug or carpeting, only the uniform, cold surface under his buttocks and against his back. The floor and the wall were probably concrete.

He kept on speaking in Spanish and then repeating every phrase in French. He could not think of any other way to prove to his kidnappers that he was not the person they thought.

"I'm not a gringo. *Je ne suis pas américain.* You can check my identification. *Vous pouvez le constater sur ma piéce d' identité.*"

There was no response. He reached into the inside pocket of his suit coat to find his papers. They weren't there, but that surprised him less than the realization that they had changed his clothes. He explored his new attire with his hands. He was now dressed in a large shirt without buttons or pockets and some very loose pants, like pajama bottoms. His feet were shod in sandals of the same material, with rope soles. The cloth in which he was dressed was plain, but not at all rough. It reminded him of the clothing hospital patients wear; then, although he had never been in jail, it reminded him of the uniforms prisoners wear. He imagined the cloth to be black, like everything else around him. Almost nostalgically, he recalled the colors of the clothing he had worn when he went out to eat with Jenkins: the navy blue of his blazer, the light yellow of his shirt, his red tie, his pants a vague shade of khaki, the bright maroon of his loafers.

A sudden realization interrupted these reminiscences. The kidnappers knew who he was. They had read it on his identity card: "M. Javier Salcedo, Deuxiéme Sécrétaire de l'Ambassade du Mexique," and in spite of that, they were keeping him locked up. Various hypotheses occurred to him immediately; as usual, he chose the most optimistic. The men who had taken him captive were obeying orders; it was someone else's job to decide what to do afterward. It was probable that the headman, the person who had conceived the kidnapping, still did not know that his minions had made a mistake. When he became aware of the mistake, he would certainly order them to set him free. Salcedo tried to convince himself that it there could not be any other explanation; after all, a Mexican diplomat was of no exchange value on the international terrorism market.

After a while, which he let pass without moving from his sitting position, he made a judgment that came as a blow to his optimism. He was thirsty, he needed to urinate, his legs were stiff; he had probably left the restaurant with Jenkins four hours ago, five, maybe more. It was strange that they had waited so long to come to take him out of there.

To allay his fears, to do something, whatever that might be, to find a way out, to hasten his liberation in some way, he leaned on the wall with both hands, and raised himself up until he was standing upright. The impossibility of seeing where he was made him dizzy, and he had to wait a while for his legs to hold him up more steadily. Then, moved by an urgent need in his lower abdomen, still leaning on the wall with one hand, he stepped away from it. With the other hand he lowered his pants to his knees, simultaneously spreading his legs to avoid falling. In that posture, which reminded him of more than one early morning on the solitary streets after a night of drinking, he urinated leisurely against the wall. This ordinary pleasure, the first he had felt in a long time, absorbed all his attention. He did not notice until it was too late that the urine had run down the floor and was wetting his feet through his sandals. With instinctive repugnance, he took a few steps back and lost his balance. Immediately he leaned forward to regain it, then straightened up his body, but his outstretched hands did not find the wall.

He almost fell. As he reeled about, he thought he felt a source of heat overhead. He raised his arms and the heat was more intense, but he couldn't touch anything. He supposed that in the ceiling, which was probably very high, there was a ventilation system, perhaps a register, from which the hot air was coming. However, other pressing concerns distracted him from his speculation. With the little self-confidence he had left, he concentrated on taking a step, two steps forward. His hands groped an emptiness so dense he could almost feel it oozing through his fingers. He stepped back. He made a right-face and moved forward again, with no better luck. He stepped back again. He did an about-face and walked forward with arms outstretched, but this was also to no avail. He had lost his only bearing in that dark world that obliterated everything.

The fear, which had not left him even for an instant since his capture, turned into panic. He felt that the darkness, wrapped around his body like a living thing, was teeming with threats that palpitated above his head, at his feet, in front of him and at his back. His immediate impulse was to run, but he did not dare take another step that might move him even farther from the wall. He felt as defenseless and alone as he had when as a child the nightmares would often wake him in the middle of the night. But now he knew that no one stronger would come to his aid. Accosted on all sides by a host of dangers that were getting closer and closer, he collapsed to the point that his knees and then his hands touched the floor. No longer in command of his actions, he fell on his side, assumed a fetal position, and cried until the tears drowned his fears.

He felt better after crying, although ashamed of his cowardice. With difficulty, he started to get up, but he stopped halfway; he had discovered that if he got up on all fours, he was less likely to trip and fall. Walking facedown, like a quadruped, he advanced a few yards. Suddenly he felt his right hand sinking into some kind of liquid and he withdrew it immediately. Once over the shock, he confirmed with relief that the sharp sensation on his skin was not a burn, as he had first thought, but a cold feeling, more unexpected than intense. Groping, he searched around the floor and finally came in contact with a concave metallic object he took to be a receptacle of some sort. He picked it up with both hands and cautiously brought it up to his face. The liquid had no odor. After hesitating for a few seconds, he dared take a sip. The taste that poured into his mouth filled him with an elemental joy. It was water.

He drank with the receptacle raised to his lips, feeling the water run down his cheeks, wetting his chest. As he placed the empty vessel on the floor, it occurred to him that somewhere there might be another with food in it. He searched around close to himself, a little further, ever more distant from the place where he had drunk the water. He did not find what he was looking for, but as he crawled around the room on all fours, he suddenly banged his head against the wall.

He experienced both a great relief at having recovered his bearings and an irrepressible anger at the lump he could feel swelling on his forehead. As he touched the swollen spot, he remembered the metallic belt they had wrapped around his head. Angrily, he tried to take it off, but once again the clawing pain proved intolerable and he had to stop. He realized the wound in the nape of his neck was more serious than he had at first thought. He imagined that pieces of his flesh had adhered to the foam rubber with which the strange bandage was attached. That thought wiped out his anger and the little confidence he had gained from getting back to the wall. Dazed by the sharp pain in his forehead and neck, he lay down to wait for it to subside. He stretched out on the floor, with his back to the wall and his face turned toward the indiscernible space of the room. His thoughts began to repeat themselves, becoming concentric. He kept asking himself about his kidnappers. Why had they taken him captive? Where had they locked him up? What were they going to do with him? Who were they? Who?

At some point he opened his eyes and saw that the cell was illuminated. It was very small, or at least that was how it looked to him in his bewildered state. Actually, it appeared a quite ordinary room, with four walls at right angles to each other. There were no windows, but except for that it could have been the bedroom in which he had slept as a child. The door was even in the same place, although it had been left ajar, and beyond it, instead of his parents' room, there was a dark hallway. Out of the shadows a man suddenly appeared, beckoning to him. Salcedo got up and walked toward him. Just as he reached the door he realized that the man calling to him was Jenkins, and at that moment he awoke.

Still startled, he tried to make out the place where the door had been. It was useless: what he saw was complete darkness; now, only in dreams were colors and light accessible to him. He could not get over the memory of Jenkins, half-hidden in the shadows of the nightmare. By now they would probably have discovered his dead body.

Accustomed to seeing the world through press reports, he imagined the story as it would be published in the evening papers: written in the grave tones of *Le Monde*, with intricate details concerning terrorism in Paris, and a precise recounting of terrorist assaults against North American diplomats since the last war, or presented scandalously on the front page of *France-Soir,* with an immense photograph of Jenkins framed by smaller ones of his wife and daughters, indignant statements by the U.S. ambassador and perhaps the hasty comments of some French minister. Perhaps his name appeared also.

The police are looking for a secretary of the Mexican embassy, Señor Javier Salcedo, who was the last person to see Mr. Jenkins alive. The owner of the restaurant where the two diplomats dined assured the police that Jenkins and Salcedo left the establishment together a little before midnight.

It was quite possible that they were looking for him. At the embassy his absence would be perplexing; his secretary would check his appointment book to see if he had an appointment in the city; she would probably read on the previous day's page, "Supper with Jenkins, 9:00 P.M., Aux délices de St. Louis." And if his name actually appeared in the story, the Mexican correspondents would surely have inflated it:

ATTACHÉ TO MEXICAN EMBASSY IN FRANCE DISAPPEARS
His Companion North American Diplomat
Stabbed to Death
French Police Suspect Mexican Diplomat Kidnapped

Perhaps someone in his family or a friend had read about it in Mexico. Perhaps they were placing a long-distance call to the embassy at this very moment.

Sadly, he thought about the world outside, about a few favorite streets, about the intimate solitude of his apartment, about his office, which he had never missed before, about a few people he loved, especially a certain woman. No one could help him. His lips and throat had again dried up, and now he was feeling his empty stomach. Judging by his hunger and thirst, which were his only reference points, a long time had gone by since he was taken captive, probably a whole day. The kidnappers were taking too long to decide what to do with him. He needed to talk to them, to make them understand that he was not the hostage they were looking for, to convince them that if they set him free he would take no action against them. He had to find a way out, some way to communicate with the outside.

He stood up facing the wall and began running his hands along its surface, looking for a hinge, a door latch, a button, any clue to a hidden lock. The darkness had become a familiar environment, within which he could get around with a certain amount of skill. He moved to his right, patiently examining every inch of the wall from top to bottom with the palms of his hands, up to where his arms could reach. The first time he raised his hands on the wall, he remembered the sensation of heat he had felt before, when he wandered about the interior of the cell, and he noticed that he now felt no change in temperature. He figured that the ventilation, the heat, or whatever it was, was probably in the middle of the ceiling or very close to it, but he discarded those conjectures he could not verify, and once again concentrated on the wall. As he advanced, the perception his meticulous hands discerned was ever the same: a flat surface, cold, uniform, continuous, with no interruptions. After a few of the same monotonous yards, Salcedo got an idea that filled him with anguish. He began to suspect that the cell was circular. Shaken, he foresaw the possibility of infinitely running along a continuous wall, unknowingly bypassing his starting point time and again. After thinking it over for a moment, he took off his shirt, spread it out on the ground next to the wall, making sure he would trip on it when he came back to that same place, and continued his search. He was satisfied, almost proud of having created a sign that would help him avoid the horrors of repetition. A little further on, as he felt around over his head, he suddenly rubbed against an object that was stuck to the wall about two yards above the floor.

His fingers avidly examined it. It was fixed to the wall by a square base, a little larger than the palm of his hand, made of a stiff material, not as cold as the concrete, maybe some kind of plastic. At the lower part of the square, there was a forked protrusion, covered in plastic, with a metal slot between the pincers that formed the fork. Higher up he felt a metal bar affixed to the plastic base by a nut and bolt that allowed it to move. The bar was long and straight, narrow enough to fit in the groove below; the opposite end was encased in a plastic cap. Salcedo constructed a visual image of the object he had touched and realized, happily, that it was a circuit breaker.

Without giving it much thought, he grabbed the metal bar by the plastic-covered end and pulled it down into the groove. Then he took his hand off the switch and waited a moment, with his blood rushing to his face. But no door opened, no blinding light suddenly turned on. Everything remained the same, except for the unexpected dizziness Salcedo attributed to his dashed hopes.

To recuperate from that bad feeling he slid down with his back to the wall. He sat as before, but now he was overwhelmed by a suspicion he had rejected until that moment. They were torturing him. They had begun by breaking him down through fear of darkness. Then, with the water that revived him, they had prolonged his resistance. And time, lengthened by confinement, had prepared him for one last torment, perhaps the meanest of all. Sooner or later it had to occur to him to look for a way out, and the kidnappers had placed a useless switch within his reach, to torture him with hope. They were toying with him. At that very moment they were probably in a room next to the cell, enjoying themselves at his expense.

While he was thinking he had wrapped his arms around his legs. Now, with his head sunk between his arms, he smelled a rancid odor coming from his armpits. His brow and his back were also sweaty. He was tired, defeated, humiliated. He had no more resources left to resist that impersonal factory that was taking him apart. In despair he yelled into the black space gravitating about him:

"That's enough. *Ça suffit.* I beg you."

Surprise stopped him from translating the last sentence. He had not heard his screams.

He tried again, still unbelieving, but no sound stimulated his eardrums. Now in anguish, he wrapped a hand around his neck and screamed again. He felt his throat vibrate on his fingers and became disconcerted. Even now he had heard nothing, absolutely nothing.

Perplexed, he at first feared that the blows to his head had left him deaf, but shortly he realized that explanation had to be false. He recalled hearing his voice just after he awakened in the dark, when he had tried to communicate with his kidnappers. He recalled the muted sound of his steps as he explored the cell. And he was sure he had heard his own heavy breathing a moment before throwing the switch. His deafness had begun immediately after.

Although associating those ideas seemed insane, he figured he had nothing left to lose. He hurriedly stood up, fully intending to disconnect the switch, but just as he rose, stretching one arm to reach it, his loss of hearing made him lose his balance. His momentum hurled him against the wall. Instinctively he looked for something to hold on to and his hand found a switch. He realized that it was open and that with the inertia of his fall, he was closing it. And he kept on falling.

He did not feel the impact against the floor. Instead of the anticipated pain in his head, his shoulders, his knees, Salcedo had an unexpected sensation of placidity. It seemed he was immersed in a lukewarm substance that made his whole body feel lethargic. Surprised, he let himself be carried along by the delights of that lethargy, until he suddenly understood. The switch he had thrown while falling was not the one he had been searching for; he himself had thrown the other one just before he was deafened. The peaceful sensation, so much like both drunkenness and slumber, had begun after activating the second switch.

Anxiously, he tried to get up, but no movement followed his efforts. He could not feel his arms or his legs. His whole body was beyond his reach. In some incomprehensible way, the circuit breaker had canceled his sense of touch. Infinitely disconsolate, he thought that there was not anything he could now do to get out of the darkness, and just then he recalled the heat source he believed he detected over his head while he was lost in the interior of the cell. That memory unchained his worst conjectures. He supposed the heat source was a lightbulb, and that it had been on the whole time. He suspected that after the kidnappers had locked him in his cell, they had thrown a switch, the first one, which was used to deprive him of sight. He reasoned that he himself, in his rush to find an exit, had thrown the other two. Finally, he tried to envision an atrocious machine that was operated by five switches attached to the victim through the metal band that he could no longer feel on the nape of his neck.

He smelled the sweat that had to be coming from his own flesh, and the bitter, dry taste of a dirty mouth reached him from somewhere. It was all he could perceive. Enclosed in a body that was no longer his, Salcedo concluded that at any moment, without his being able to touch them, hear them, or see them, his executioners would come to throw the two missing switches once and for all.

MORENTE
Rosina Conde

to Ramírez Avendaño, in memoriam

What is more, we had discovered that the ocean could produce
what no artificial synthesis had ever managed to reproduce: a perfect
human body . . .
In a certain sense, [the ocean] has taken into consideration
desires hidden in some secret corner of our minds. Perhaps it was
sending us . . . gifts.
. . . but to leave was to renounce a certain possibility, of ridicu-
lously low probability, perhaps only imaginary . . . So, did I have to
go on living here, among the furnishings, the things that we had both
touched, in the air that she had once breathed? In the name of what?
—Stanislav Lem, *Solaris*

SOLITUDE MOVES ME TO WRITE: THE LONELINESS OF THE CITY, THE HOUSE, THE
furniture, and objects, the pen itself. It's interesting, I was looking for a cigarette, but just the same, I picked up my purse and took out my pen, and
here I am now, sitting at the window in my study, watching the waves breaking on the rocks below the cliffs, bringing the lights of the bay to life. I often
sit here, leaning against the window frame, watching and listening to the
angry pounding of the water. Sometimes the gulls fly above it, depending on
the season, and play in the foam the waves leave behind as they ebb and flow.
At this hour, when the tide is highest, especially under this full moon, the
sound is clearer, more transparent, and more serene. I have spent hours
observing those blue-green waves and those jagged rocks that emerge like
stalagmites encrusted with mussels and barnacles; some are twisted into
grotesque shapes like Gothic drawings; others are smooth, or just plain flat
and gray-green.

Without realizing it, I'm here thinking of Morente, that boy who showed
up a few months ago at twelve noon and stood in the open doorway, staring

at my legs as I read the newspaper in the living room. He hesitated a bit before deciding to speak to me; then he came in nervously and said simply, "Hello," as he sat down next to me.

"I've just moved into the house next door," he told me after looking at me for a while, "This place is nice," he added.

I smiled and looked into his eyes, round, deep eyes with the longest lashes I'd ever seen, and I watched him move from the chair to the window and from the window to the chair.

"I haven't introduced myself," he said ten minutes after coming in, speaking to me and walking around the room, "My name is Morente and I'm from Tijuana; I've come to study biological sciences."

I spoke to him for the first time. I offered my hand and said:

"Pleased to meet you. I'm Marina, from Mexicali."

He smiled happily when he heard my name; he stood in front of the window again, watching the waves, repeating it. I laughed girlishly.

"What a pretty name," he said, "It fascinates me!"

"Yeah, I'm sure you find it enchanting . . . what's more, it even drives you utterly mad," I said, mocking his pretentiousness.

"Yes, it does drive me mad," he declared staring at me seriously; then he changed his tone and invited me to have a beer.

"I have to study," I answered. "I'm taking an exam next Friday."

"Well, you still have time to prepare. We can celebrate, can't we?"

"Celebrate?" I asked, surprised.

Without giving me time to react, he concluded:

"Perfect! Then I'll go for the beer. What do you think, sunshine, heat, beer, and a lot of time to talk. What more can I offer you?"

I laughed again. For a few minutes I could not get over my surprise, and I stared at his legs like an idiot as he took off running; I thought about his bare arms as they disappeared into a beat-up sports car. He was in great shape. His neck was thick and solid, his back wide, triangular, and his arms, . . . his arms were like a stevedore's, strong and nicely rounded, the veins crisscrossing his muscles, the hairs sun bleached very blond.

Morente returned an hour later. He had not only bought beer, but also meat, charcoal, vegetables, and flour tortillas.

"Let's have a big party!" he said excitedly, "I have a barbecue and folding chairs on my terrace."

We spent a few hours on his terrace talking and looking at the horizon marked by the sea; we played backgammon, went running on the beach, and picked mussels from the cliff. Morente laughed at me when he realized that I had never dared climb down from it.

"Marina!" he said. "Here you are, named for the sea, and afraid of a few silly waves! If you really knew the ocean, this wouldn't scare you!"

But my sunburned back stung when I felt the lash of the water and its foam, and I became truly frightened by the undertow, which seemed intent upon yanking us off the rocks. Nevertheless, I felt protected when I realized how strong his arms were; they helped me climb back to the top. There we lay, contemplating the horizon marked by the ocean and that hot orange sun setting right in front of us.

Morente's muscular back shone in the light of the moon. The waves, now serenely at our feet, lulled us. I felt relaxed and excited at the same time; my thighs contracted and my heart did somersaults in my breast. Under his body, I gasped for air, sinking into the sand. Yet, I felt happy in spite of the pain down inside me. I started laughing when I felt myself penetrated. It was an almost indefinable pain. I imagined I was a balloon bursting in the air. A few minutes later, we lay still: our breathing slowed. Our sight, suspended in the darkness, discovered the aura of the moon. Morente was a gift of the ocean that, now and then, wet our feet, making us shiver. Morente the vision, the ghost, the apparition; Morente idealized, desired, sought after; Morente materialized as a being, as a man, as the infinite, looked at me from the depth of his eyes, those eyes of indefinite color, whose tones changed with the position of the moon. It was like seeing the ocean through a kaleidoscope of configurations of seaweed and marine stones. His breathing transported me to the breaking of the waves that I am even now hearing from my window. I felt afraid and I told him so:

"Afraid . . . ? Of what?" he asked me, surprised.

"Of your leaving," I answered without thinking, "that you'll disappear just as suddenly as you arrived."

"I am from the sea," he responded, nearly asleep. "I am from the sea," he repeated, murmuring, "and someday I will return to it: I'll go in walking, struggling against the tide, and I'll nail myself with that moon when it is hurled from the sky, and I'll sink with it."

And then he fell asleep.

The drizzle awoke us. The seagulls walked around us without paying us any mind. Our bodies stretched, reached for each other thirstily, smelling of salt. We were still damp when we got up. We picked up the bags of mussels and walked slowly. We got to the house full of joy and optimism. We washed the mussels and put them to boiling, and, without actually agreeing to, we began our day as though we had known each other for a long time, as though we had lived all our lives there, and the days passed in the everyday activities of a marriage as ancient as life itself.

The next week Marco and Antonio, two students of mine, came to invite us on an excursion to Maneadero. The plan was to visit La Bufadora, near Ensenada, and then camp a bit farther south to fish and have a good time over the weekend. At first I decided not to go because I had exams and Morente's arrival had cut short my study time; but then I agreed that visiting La Bufadora with him would be the best thing that could happen to me, since no one in the world appreciated the sea more than he. It seemed he was part of it: his skin always felt mossy to my touch and I found his briny perspiration terribly attractive. When I said I would go with them to La Bufadora, Morente danced like a child who had just gotten his favorite toy. If I remember right, if my memory isn't playing tricks on me, he crossed my terrace and leaped up to his, excited by the prospect of going to Maneadero. He jumped three times after leaping over the low wall. I watched his tennis shoes dance from one side to the other, with the stripes on his socks forming colored waves in the air. He went into his house running and screaming that he loved me, that he would love me from wherever he was. I, too, went up to my bedroom to change, running up the stairs, and my students waited for us in the living room. We left at nine in the morning.

The day was dazzling. The sky was so clear we enjoyed a perfect view of the bay, with its catamarans and mountains. Now I was glad I had decided to go, and I thought it would be even better to study after relaxing on the trip. I finally understood why my students preferred to travel rather than locking themselves up to study before exams. It was hot; the air was rather suffocating. During the trip, I drove in silence. Morente sang. I pondered the fact that neither of us had bothered to speak about anything other than ourselves. If I had told him that I had a son almost his age, he might have gotten scared, and until that moment, I had not thought about it because, although he insisted on saying he loved me, I kept my distance. I thought it wouldn't last long. He seemed preoccupied only with the present. Just the same, I wasn't afraid anymore, because since Morente arrived I'd begun to rediscover a number of truths about myself that I had completely forgotten. As a matter of fact, until that very moment, I had not thought about Felipe, my son, whom I saw two or three times a semester. I realized I had become too egotistic, that all I thought about were my examinations, my classes, my lonely widow habits. It was only then that I realized I was living in a kind of bell jar that isolated me from my own, which first of all cut me off from myself.

My students arrived first. When we caught up with them, they were happily getting soaked by La Bufadora's geyser spray, calling to a seal swimming among the rocks. Some children laughed and others cried when they saw the fragmentation of the water, preceded by the imposing growl. Now I was thankful that I had decided to go and to forget my doctoral exams and university courses completely.

My memory fails me sometimes: I was so immersed in myself that day that I only remember the roar of the water and the swirling current. And him.

We left about four o'clock. Morente and my students still had to drive farther south and camp, and didn't want to be overtaken by nightfall, so all we ate were some tostadas and fish tacos before leaving. On the way back, I contemplated the solitude I'd lived in for ten years, what it meant. I no longer remembered that I had once lived in the company of another person. Since Heriberto died, I'd had no interest in sharing my thoughts with anyone. I had lived only with Felipe, who also didn't seem worried about the absence of his father. We both had taken it calmly, as though Heriberto had stepped out to buy cigarettes or tortillas and death had never been among us. We simply didn't bring the subject up again, and we locked ourselves in our own time and space, and when we both grew up, each of us went his and her way without blame, without tears or lamentations. The day Felipe left, I picked up some castanets and started playing them. The dry sound produced by the wood accompanied me for a few days, and then came a long silence. Silence!

The next day, in the afternoon, Marco and Antonio returned without Morente. They had spent the night drinking beer and singing around a fire pit, and at dawn, when the moon was about to set, Morente said he was going for a walk. Marco and Antonio crept into their tent and did not awaken until midday. But Morente did not come back. The most intriguing fact is that his things were not there either. At first they thought they'd been robbed sometime during the morning, but everything was untouched, except for Morente's gear. There was no sign that anyone, including Morente, had been there with them. They even thought they might have dreamed it all up, and they had me repeat step by step what we had done the day before, just to convince themselves that they hadn't been hallucinating.

This time I could not take it calmly. This time the bell cracked and shattered. Then I started screaming from my gut, crying and pacing around the house, tearing my hair. Then my anguish rose from my womb to my breasts and my lungs could no longer fit anywhere. Then I felt anger and rage and impotence. Then I learned what solitude and silence really were. Then mind and body crashed into each other in a convulsion totally out of my control, and I saw myself, as I see myself now, from afar, completely unhinged and out of my mind, leaving myself like the waves under the cliff I hear from my window.

"It isn't possible," Marco said, trying to get me under control, "Morente's played a bad joke on us."

"But, I wonder what time he came back for his things?" Antonio asked himself. "He didn't have a car; how could he carry them? He was carrying very heavy gear. There was no salmon in the bag and it was still sealed with tape . . . We dreamed it . . . It was a collective dream . . ."

"A collective dream," Marco repeated, intrigued and not very convinced, "Yes, a collective dream."

We searched for him for days on end. They dragged the coast with special equipment to see if he had gotten tangled in the kelp, and my friends in marine sciences dove under the rocks where he had last been seen. The police inspected the beach area to make sure my students hadn't buried him. Nothing. Morente's body never showed up and no one ever came to Ensenada to claim it. I went to Tijuana to try and locate his family, but they did not exist.

The first Sunday of the next month, when the landlord came to collect my rent, I asked him about the renter who had occupied the neighboring house. He looked at me, surprised.

"That house has not been rented for six months, Señora," he answered.

Of course, I didn't believe him, and after paying him the rent, I went to snoop around Morente's patio, but it was untouched, with six months of dust and dirt on it. I could not find any evidence that the house had been inhabited: no sign of Morente on the floor or on the walls, no sign of me or of his personal things. I even got to the point of believing it had been a dream, a marvelous dream that I had loved so much that I wanted it to be true.

After the inquiry I had to go to Mexicali to visit my family and rest due to the stress of the search. I could not cry, nor laugh: Morente's absence had sunk me into indifference; I had lost my desire to feel, hear, and smell, and my house irritated me because there I was alone with his presence saturating the walls that were turning yellow and green with moss. I had come to hate the sea so much that Mexicali inspired a morbid pleasure in me, with its look of being a dry ocean, with that marine dryness so its own, and that pitiless sun that absorbed liquids to the point of stealing our sweat from us, and our tears. Although later I discovered that I had no reason to cry, because I realized that it had not been a dream, and that Morente had actually been there . . . ,

125

because I still have his tracks on my body and still perceive his briny, humid odor, and feel his presence at the window in the living room and in my bed, and his breath in those blue-green waves crashing against the rocks at the bottom of the cliff . . .

OLGA, OR THE DARKEST MAMBO
Mauricio Montiel

And let me go on drinking
the unquenchable thirst of the night.
—José Ángel Valente

EVERY TIME OLGA TAKES A BREATH, IT IS AS THOUGH AN IDOL WITH HARD thighs and prehistoric breasts were suddenly breathing, as though someone had put a huge, dark lung into that soaring figure, as though a savage beast had slipped into the Club Antillano from who knows what tropics hidden in the meridians of memory, as though the night had materialized as a woman and her breath were tortured by too many centuries of tobacco and moons, as though Olga herself were the night and she were having trouble breathing through all those stars she had encrusted in her throat. Olga inhales and the dance-hall faithful feel themselves being absorbed, sucked in by a bellows that obliges them to abandon the amber refuge of the rum momentarily and go track down the source of that primordial respiration, that antsy sensation tearing at their soul, the desire for a female. Olga exhales and every patron reaches back to the nape of his neck to grasp the nails caressing him, dying to find a mouth that can account for that gust of wind blowing down his back, groping in the half-light, flapping like a butterfly near his ear. At the front of the hall, on the stage bathed in almost blood-red lights, the musicians again start up that rhythm that tears down the borders between body and body, and everything goes back to normal. Midnight curls into the sweaty embrace of the trumpets, drums, timbales, and maracas, of single men drunk with solitude and girls hunting fat wallets. The Club Antillano pulsates, heart of the city wearing its weekend clothes.

Olga takes pleasure in inhaling the smoke of the Marlboro that someone's fingers have placed in the purple corner of her mouth, and coughs huskily, and her hacking is the signal the drummer in the band was awaiting to begin whipping the air with his drumsticks. She takes a drink of the rum and coke one of the waiters has brought her, as always, on the house on Fridays, Olga, nice and strong the way you like it, but what's the matter with you, Olga, we noticed you've been depressed and exhausted since you came in, Olga, since the gentleman who's now dancing with that curvaceous blonde paid for your ticket and then took off, left you here, forgot you here. Maybe he noticed the wrinkles your forty years (is it really forty, Olga, not even one more or less?) have distributed about your face, the crags that not even sixty minutes putting on makeup in front of the mirror can disguise. Maybe he found out that the obsidian black of your hair is only possible thanks to the dye that helps you hide the gray a little; or perhaps he noticed the very dark circles under your eyes, how dull your eyes must be for the light to die when it hits them, the gesture of perennial nostalgia that grows shadows under the blush of your cheeks. And what about your figure, Olga, all the age that has been accumulating in your flesh like some kind of grease out of control, your silhouette, Olga, sheathed in that imitation satin dress with its seams about to burst, your uniform for going hunting in the Friday night jungle. And your shoes with heels worn down by so many streets, Olga, by so many dance floors at the edge of dawn, and like a jolt, the pain that flashes across your gums, Olga, a lightning bolt rending your teeth, anxiety piercing the driest place on your tongue.

Olga takes pleasure in inhaling the smoke of the Marlboro that someone's fingers, now lost on the soft neck of a blonde, placed in the purple corner of her mouth. Not even the rum and coke can quench her sudden thirst, the trembling that vibrates across her mouth from side to side. And because of that, her gaze becomes sharp; for a second her eyes seem to flower like two brilliant poppies; her tongue swells, grows, palpitating to the beat of the sounds the musicians are pouring out. It's time for the mambo, Olga's religion, sacred impulse that inflames her veins. As she rises from her seat, she lets one of her shoulder straps slip down her arm, in time to the beat. She isn't wearing a bra, her breasts hang like two ancient fruit, but it's mambo time, the rhythm that lights up the shadows and makes the dead speak, and who cares about all the rest, the looks that accompany her to the dance floor, the applause of the waiters, the wolf whistles of the bouncers posted at the entrance, the insufferable thirst consuming her throat. Nothing matters now that Olga knows that Sebastian is waiting for her in a dark corner: Sebastian, her trustworthy partner every Friday since the beginning of time, Sebastian, the widower in his fifties who has found his most faithful companion in the dance; Sebastian, the only man with whom Olga has been able to communicate through the tribal code of the mambo, and there is Sebastian's beige felt hat, there are Sebastian's salt-and-pepper mustache, suspenders, and plaid pants, there is the dance floor, completely empty and surrounded by hungry eyes, here is the saliva Olga swallows as if she were swallowing a cascade of fire, a torrent of lava.

The musicians smile behind their instruments, submerging themselves in a tide of conga drums and brass. This is your moment, Olga, this and no other, princess of cosmetic wrinkles, magnificent cow, witch. The dance floor awaits you like an open hand, Olga, take it by storm, make it groan under your worn-down heels, tear it up, split it in two, destroy it. Sebastian awaits you like a door opening to the night, Olga, see him quiver as the music climbs up his legs, up his abdomen, up his chest, up to his neck, Olga, always that neck that makes your thirst more painful; approach him slowly, cautiously, Olga, slowly look him in the eye and let him look at you, let his pupils slide down your shoulders and recognize them and then, yes, Olga, throw yourself into the vertigo of the mambo, hurl yourself with every muscle in your body into that tropical whirlpool that sucks in everything, that demolishes everything, that cancels everything. Feel your hips moving faster, your sleepwalking hunter's outfit tenses under your waist until it's about to burst, and your ass, Olga, how your ass shakes the musk-filled air around it, how it adapts to the sway dictated from the stage and trembles and shakes foreshadowing an immense earthquake, the shattering of dawn into a million pieces that already furrow your gums. Move, Olga, shake your hips from one end to another, from east to west, throw them to the eyes devouring them, Olga, transform yourself into the goddess the customers seek in the fumes of the alcohol, erect yourself into the greatest totem of the night but by moving only your hips, Olga, shaking your hips without seeing Sebastian, without joining Sebastian, without melding into Sebastian; like that, Olga, just like that, the two of you separated, the two of you wrapped in the chrysalis of the dance, Olga and Sebastian together in the transparent cocoon woven by the mambo until the end of everything, until the musicians burst in an avalanche of trumpets but faster, Sebastian and Olga, more frantic movement at the waist, there Olga's ass, that's it, there Sebastian's hips, that's it, just like that, magically like that, the atmosphere exploding to the last sounds of the agonizing tropic that inundates the Club Antillano, just like that.

The audience breaks into applause and whistles when the band stops playing, dog-tired. Olga and Sebastian stand panting in the middle of the dance floor, hot, wrapped in the red drunkenness of the lights, not touching, vaguely satisfied. In the air, in the ethyl spirits of the customers, a few filaments of music still sparkle. The ovation lasts for a few seconds that are like centuries for Olga; she bursts into her accustomed, euphoric Friday night laugh, feeling the familiar pain in her canines, in her tongue drowning in a tenacious thirst. Sebastian doffs his hat, taking a bow, wiping his hand across his wet brow, adjusting his suspenders; he turns toward Olga and offers her a toothy smile that sums up all those years of dancing, all those smiles that have substituted for any physical contact, words are futile, the toast to the beginning of a relationship that cannot go beyond a casual brush of their fingers, an obligatory kiss on the cheek. Olga understands, and because of it she accepts his leaving the dance floor alone as always, drenched as always, going back to a table navigating in the half-light as always. The singer in the band announces that we'll be back with you after a brief break, ladies and gentlemen, don't despair, keep on enjoying this, your Club Antillano. The musicians come down from the stage, eager to get to the bar awaiting them with open bottles. The sound system begins spilling out heavy salsa that dampens the glow of the applause, firing up the liquor that circulates in the blood of the night people. In a wink the dance floor is populated by thighs trying to meld with the immense pulse of the city. The Club Antillano, soul of the dying week, goes on throbbing.

And Olga, intuiting that the Friday hunt has already begun, that a pair of eyes are glued to the rise and fall of her heavy breathing, clears a path for herself through the dancers. She moves toward her solitary table, her nipples erect, her thirst deeper than ever, her shoulder strap slipping again, to reveal the curve of her left breast, just a hint of the coarse hair growing in her armpit. She sits down, languidly, with the eyes that are following her now softly rubbing her belly, the triangular insinuation of her pubis. Almost immediately a waiter places a stiff rum and coke, Olga, a Havana Club, in front of you, the gentleman in the blue coat, yes, the blond guy at that table wants to know if it would bother you if he came and sat with you, Olga, tell him it wouldn't, not in the least, one doesn't even ask that question, what is he waiting for, Olga, queen of the powdered eyelids, miraculous elephant, witch. When he comes up to you, reeling, with a beer poking through his fingers, Olga, as soon as you identify his gaze drunkenly running over your shoulders and beauty marks and you realize that he has not taken it off you from the time the mambo began, the world began, Olga, wet your lips with your tongue so your words will come out damp as you invite him to sit, so your thirst will be masked a bit with saliva. Look him over from head to foot as he takes the seat next to you, slightly nervous, Olga, carefully study his face tanned by the suns of his twenty-five to thirty years; thank him kindly for the drink and ask him what he does, what someone as handsome as he is doing around this rumba joint; smile warmly as you hear him babbling in a faraway, foreign accent, saying how well you dance, that you are the most beautiful mulatta in this whole joint, that he would love to dance with you that delicious bolero the trumpets are blowing now. He lets his shaky hand wrap around your waist as you go toward the dance floor, Olga, breathe deeply the perfume of youth emanating from his neck and become drunk; nibble him, digging your teeth in just a little, Olga, enjoying the spasm that flashes through your gums, feeling how his fingers begin to trace circular caresses across your ass, Olga; how your nails slowly become entangled in his hair, how the blood travels loudly through the vein beating in his throat. Hear him whisper in your ear with his hoarse voice that he's here on business, that he's staying at the Caribe on the top floor, that he would pay you a large tip if you will accompany him to his room with a view of the city, to a bed with fresh, crisp sheets. Of course you must accept the offer, Olga, accept it, girl of so many broken moons, ancient rumba dancer, she-wolf; you know well that once you're locked in at the top of the hotel, naked and very sweaty at the top of the town, while his tongue explores the secrets of your pores and the dawn covers the picture window with its neon neurosis, you will be able to give vent to your thirst until you slake it, Olga, slake it, let the pain make your real teeth protrude and sink them into the neck that opens before you like an orchid, Olga, stick your millennial fangs into that tender skin and drink, Olga, drink the youth that bubbles forth, drink the blond shriek that rends the pillows, drink the city and the whole night, Olga, unquenchable thirst, kiss tainted red, countess dancing the darkest mambo of all with your mouth.

ISAIAH VII, 14

Ethel Krauze

> Therefore the Lord himself shall give you a sign:
> Behold, a virgin shall conceive, and bear a son,
> and shall call his name Immanuel.

THE ANXIETY HAD BEGUN IN NOVEMBER. THE TELEPHONE WOULD RING AND Jana would run to answer it, laughing and shrieking. Her husband would look up from the newspaper, awaiting the signal. No. Not yet. They each returned to what they were doing without speaking to each other.

On the twenty-second of December they were forced to decide. There was no other way. They were eating when Guite asked:

"Where do you plan to spend Christmas Eve?"

Boris took his eyes from his newspaper; Jana gulped down an enormous mouthful and said, without looking at her daughter:

"At Sanborn's."

"Sanborn's!" Guite repeated, almost to herself. "But it's a plastic cafeteria! Why not a more . . . a less . . . ? Hasn't anyone invited you out?"

Jana shook her head calmly.

"What about the Sanchez Bulneses? Or the Ordoñezes?" Guite asked.

Jana shook her head, devouring crackers.

"I'm going with you," said Guite, after a few awkward moments.

Jana smiled. Boris raised his eyes from the newspaper again, while Guite tried to offer a not-too-clear explanation:

"That idiot Juan asked his mother to invite me, and she made a face, and I told him I can't stand his mother's sneers. I don't need those people to get through Christmas . . ."

"We'll do quite nicely, you'll see," Jana was quick to say. "I already asked about the price, which is decent, and there'll be a band, too. We can walk there, after all it's so close, and that way we avoid the problems with the car. No, we've thought it over and it's best, isn't that so, Boris? I'm going to wear my darling little blue dress."

Boris folded the newspaper. He got up silently and went to take his daily nap.

At nine sharp they entered Sanborn's. They had waited for the phone to ring until the last minute. The day before they did not go out, fearing the maids would not be able to take the message properly. They had hounded the maids with questions for weeks. The morning of the twenty-fourth Jana was in a good mood. She made the reservations and told everyone that they could cancel at the last minute, although they would lose the deposit, just a few more pesos after all, a few pesos more, a few pesos less, what's the difference? And they were such close friends that they could very well have placed them last on their list.

The day was slipping by. It went quickly.

"It's that the Licenciado Bulnes's mother died, they're in mourning, surely they aren't going to celebrate. Who knows what has happened to the Ordoñezes this year! What if we call them?" Jana said, putting on her blue dress.

Boris was watching television, stretched out on the bed. Guite got all decked out. She was determined.

"All right, Mama, stop feeling sorry for yourself. We don't need anyone."

They overdid their good-bye to the maids. Boris joked with them, gave them money, hugged them.

"Have a very merry Christmas, girls!" he said patting them on the back. They laughed, turning red in the face.

Jana repeatedly told them to watch the house. Guite's eye began to twitch when Maria surreptitiously made the sign of the cross on her forehead.

The noisy crowd at Sanborn's perked them up. It was still early and many people were doing their last-minute shopping at the tobacco counter and even at the pharmacy. The tables were almost all empty. But the comings and goings of perfumed coats in the aisles was promising: the fragrances of Avon, Max Factor, and Palmolive. They were enough to make Christmas Eve aromatic. They sat down right in the middle of the dining area. They wanted to see everything. They cheerfully noticed the band instruments: cymbals, drums, and an electric guitar, next to the kitchen door. The music would begin later. In front of a reflector with tiny colored crystals a small silver tree rotated on the corner of the bar. Cardboard angels hung from the cash register and from the pancake trays in the display case.

Before they ordered anything, the waitress plopped down a little punch-filled piñata in front of each of them.

"Oh, it's a little cold," said Jana, tasting it, "but it's tasty."

"What pretty little piñatas!" said Guite.

"We're leaving early because it's very dangerous walking around on the streets tonight," said Boris.

"Oh, Papa, we just got here!"

They savored the frozen punch, overhearing random conversations that excited them:

"Paco, hurry up or we'll be late!"

"What a nice little computerized watch!"

"We put up a gigantic tree. Absolutely heavenly!"

"No, Aunt Gucha's codfish is a disaster . . ."

"How's this lighter for Rogelio?"

"Compadre, compadre! Hey, shake a leg! Pall Mall, a pack. What do you mean there aren't any?"

You tell me you need ice now, daughter, at this hour? Where am I going to find ice?"

"Hurry, get in line."

"No, no, no blue ribbons on a Santa Claus!"

They watched the resplendent treks from one counter to another, the gift boxes, the dresses, the shiny shoes. Even the waitresses looked all dressed up tonight, in their stiff traditional Tehuana uniforms, tennis shoes, and rococo aprons. Even the napkins made to look like little patchwork tablecloths rustled, fragrant with chlorine and starch. They suddenly noticed that some familiar faces were greeting them. It was the Rosenbergs approaching their table. They tried to hide, to no avail.

"Boris, Janeleh! Vot's going on!" said Mr. Rosenberg, wheezing.

"My daughter here . . . she dragged us out to have coffee," stammered Boris. Jana smiled mechanically at Mrs. Rosenberg.

Guite could not resist the opportunity:

"Did you come here to celebrate Christmas, too?"

"Oy, veh!" exclaimed Mrs. Rosenberg, placing her hand on her breast.

"Dat is not a holiday of ours," Mr. Rosenberg said, lowering his voice and bending down to unleash his acid breath on Guite.

"Oh . . . can one ask what it is you did come for?"

"Oy, oy yout', yout,' dat's der yout' of today, Boris, not so?" said Mr. Rosenberg with a great desire to disappear.

Boris and Jana smiled, shaking their heads, with a great desire to make the Rosenbergs disappear, a desire the latter fulfilled by sitting at the farthest table from them.

"That's all I needed," Guite sighed. "Hypocrites!"

"Well, we did not come here to talk about that," said Jana, considering the incident closed. Boris growled:

"Just remember we're leaving early."

The menu offered stuffed turkey or codfish. Jana wanted both. They discussed asking for half orders. Guite wanted to know if they included *romeritos,* the closest thing to potato pancakes, on any of their menus. At that very moment Sonia showed up, a little tipsy, throwing her arms around her parents' shoulders.

"A merry, merry, merry Christmas, my beloved parental units!"

"Darling girl!" they cried out.

"Maria told me you were here and I said no, before I go to my bash I had to drop by and have a drink with you. Why didn't you go out with the Sanchez Bulneses?"

"Sit down."

"They're waiting for me, and I told them not to start the litany without me, because, you know, it's going to be all formal! With little candles, a piñata, and the whole nine yards. Can you imagine? I get to carry the Baby Jesus!"

Boris, who was sipping his punch, choked on a plum pit. Guite trembled. Sonia and she hated each other as only sisters can. But she couldn't resist her curiosity:

"With a litany and everything? Where, where's that?" she asked.

"At some guy's house. Well, let's drink to one helluva Christmas!"

"Well . . . Merry Christmas!" said Jana raising her punch cup.

"All right all ready," Boris growled.

"Oh, Papa," Guite simpered.

"Oh, Boris," said Jana.

"Well, I don't know if it's merry for you, but it is for me," Sonia got up, tossing her cape over her shoulders, "So, *ciao, ciao!* Have a good time! And, here's to your health," she said, tasting her sister's punch. "God, that's disgusting!"

"Look out, it's very danger . . . the street . . . the time," Boris had barely enough time to sputter, as her clicking heels made for the door under Guite's withering gaze.

Jana decided to have the turkey. She got Boris to order the codfish so they could share his portion. Guite insisted on having the *romeritos,* but they didn't have them on the menu. They tried to catch the headwaiter's eye, and they realized that now there was almost no one there. It was ten o'clock at night. The waitresses, unabashed, chatted in little groups as their few clients begged for service.

"Be r-i-i-ight there!" they cried disdainfully. "Just a m-i-i-nute!"

The turkey was dry. Jana tried to talk to the headwaiter so they would exchange it for the codfish, but there was no sign of him.

"Never mind, I'll give you mine," said Boris.

"Oh, no, why? I have to talk to the headwaiter."

"He's probably getting drunk in the kitchen," said Guite.

"So what, he should be here right now. Miss!"

137

The young woman waiting on them was having supper behind the counter.

"Let it go," Boris insisted.

"Okay, I know, let me have a little of your sauce."

They went through the whole routine at a leisurely pace. Each of them surreptitiously cast furtive glances around the restaurant. Now the only people left were the Rosenbergs, who were eating in their corner of the room without looking at each other. Over there a guy was drinking alone, staring at the wall. Two men in trench coats were at the cash register paying their bill.

The musicians appeared. Guite brightened up. They played "Feliz Navidad," heavy on the cymbals. Then they applauded themselves. Jana immediately began humming "Silent Night," and the musicians played it in her honor.

"My, how pretty and how sad," said Jana, squinting.

"All right, already," said Boris, squirming in his chair on pins and needles.

"Why are we fooling ourselves, Papa?" Guite said, tapping her plate with her fork. "We came to celebrate Christmas. All our lives we've done it on the sly, or so we said, and today, when no one invited us over, we're pretending it's just another day."

"Well, I'll be . . . that's it, let's go," said Boris, banging his plate louder.

"We did not come here to fight, please," Jana said with a tired smile on her face.

"No, Mama, but it's just that, damn it, I'm tired of feeling guilty. And besides, Papa is a liar. The other day he celebrated the Christmas *posada* in the garage with the doormen. He even broke the piñata!"

"I couldn't refuse, now could I?" They're very good people, very humble, I truly respect those people . . ."

"Don't pretend, Papa, you were happy, you wanted to, just as I have always wanted to. When we were little girls you and Mama would go out with the Sanchez Bulneses or the Ordoñezes and leave us alone with Maria, with the maids, with very good people in the kitchen, good enough for us, while you went to the big party, oh yes. And on the next day we were the only girls in the world who didn't get gifts."

"But we have *pesach* and the *afikomen* for the children, which is like a gift," Jana said.

"That's some bullshit you don't even believe in."

"My dear child!" Boris screamed.

"I'm grown up, Papa, and now you're going to hear me out. I always wanted to be Maria's daughter to celebrate Christmas with a Nativity scene, the Child Jesus and the tree and everything, and not feel like an intruder in this life."

"Why, we did let you put up a tree . . ."

"Oh, but next to the gas storage tank, so you couldn't see it from the street, and you said it was for Maria and you both sure helped hang the ornaments. But no lights, not that, because they burned at night and were proof that . . ."

"Never mind her, Jana, she doesn't know what she's talking about."

"Of course I know, Papa, I'm the one who suffered."

"You haven't suffered anything."

"Oh, don't tell me you're going to bring up the concentration camps, because I'll puke."

"Why are you talking about that on this night?" said Jana, "Your turkey is getting cold."

"You never want to talk about anything, Mama, and this crap tastes awful."

"I'll be goddamn . . ." Boris murmured signaling inexistent waitresses to bring the bill. The musicians played "Singing in the Rain," lazily, between bites of their *tortas*. The Rosenbergs had disappeared.

"You won't believe it, but I don't want to leave yet," said Guite resolutely.

"Wait until we finish, Boris, it's early."

Boris tried to contain himself. They ate dessert in silence. The solitary guy made faces as though he wanted to cry, to laugh. Some of the waitresses had taken off their uniforms. They watched the clock continuously.

"The truth is every holiday has its own thing," Jana finally said, "When we were in Israel, you should have seen the *Pesach*, Guite. Remember, Boris?"

"Over there, you said it," Guite answered rudely. "But it so happens that we're in Mexico, that I was born here, and I live here. Why don't you tell me all about China and its holidays?"

"Because, my darling daughter, it isn't the same."

"I don't see any difference: foreign countries."

"One's refuge is one's own."

"What refuge? Always and forever at war."

"For us, daughter, to defend us."

"Of course. We matter so much to them! And how they take care of us and love us! The whole damned year I spent there they treated me like a Mexican, what I mean is, like a Third World lowlife, like a second-rate foreigner. Oh, but here they treat me like a Jew, that is, like the villain of the story. I don't know what I am any more. I have to hide from everyone."

"Lower your voice," said Boris, irritated.

"I've had it with that! No, no, I won't lower it. First you send me over there to 'regain my historical identity,' which means, 'so she'll find a circumcised husband,' and since I won't play the game, they bring me back to see if they can fix me up with a stocking maker from a nice Jewish neighborhood like the Tecamachinsky. And it doesn't work! I must be damaged goods."

"You are ungrateful, we sent you so you would get to know the place. Not everyone has that privilege," said Jana, turning red.

"Well I know it now and I prefer the lowlifes, as you call them. I like Juan and he's a *goy,* a *shkotz,* of the Holy Roman Catholic faith, and devoted to the Virgin of Guadalupe!"

Boris pounded the dishes in front of him and strung together curses in Russian, English, Yiddish, Spanish, and what might even pass for Hebrew.

"Look, my darling, you'll pardon me for saying so," said Jana slowly, "but Juan's mother doesn't seem to like you. Don't you see that you can't forget what you are?"

"I don't give a damn about his mother! I'll run off with him whenever I want!" Guite exploded.

"Don't be crude," Jana screamed, "and don't yell, they're listening. We came to celebrate Christmas!"

"Damn it, shut up already!" Boris cut in.

"Well, not Christmas, but we did come to be happy!"

"What happiness! Always in secret, always halfway!" Guite said, opening her arms to encompass the desolate tables.

"The hell with this! Let's go, it's dangerous," said Boris, getting up from the table, crumpling his napkin.

"Don't be paranoid! You both have the crematorium ovens stuck in the back of your brains."

"Respect your dead, stupid girl, you are living because of them," said Boris, his fist hitting the table.

"I don't live for the dead! I want to live! I want to live! I'm sick of skeletons, of numbers tattooed even on people's tongues, of flocks of poor wretches who go to the slaughterhouse singing, of soap made of hair and children's skin, of shallow graves and hands sticking out of the muck . . . !"

"God! When another Hitler comes along . . ." sobbed Jana, covering her mouth.

"Fuck another Hitler!" Guite yelled, out of her mind.

Her father's slap shook her. Jana threw herself on him.

"The check, in the name of God, the check!"

The drunk belched stridently, asleep on the table. They looked at one another, paralyzed. No one. There were no waitresses left. The band had disappeared. They moved toward the cashier like statues. They paid and left.

Three foggy statues seemed to float by in slow motion, trembling in the silence. Guite sobbed, covering herself with her scarf. The whistling of the night watchman on his bicycle sounded down the street, in the distance. Jana started talking to herself:

"All I wanted was a good Christmas Eve . . . . or rather, no, yes, yes, that is what I wanted, a *noche buena* . . ."

They were walking half a yard away from each other. The cold was sharp.

Boris couldn't help himself. He slapped his hand with his fist. He stopped in front of his daughter, took her face in his hands and kissed her hard on the forehead, choked up with tenderness. She embraced him. Jana joined them, putting her arms around them, smiling. And you could hear their voices a block away, singing "Feliz Navidad! Feliz Navidad!" out in the dangers of the night.

SELF-LOVE
Enrique Serna

to Mauricio Peña

WHEN GERTRUDE THE WAITER TOLD ME THAT MARINA OLGUÍN THE REAL
Marina Olguín had just arrived at the Marabunta Club accompanied by two
gentlemen I thought that Carlos and Luciano had invented the story of the surprise to get me to go to the joint where they put on the drag queen shows but
before going on stage I took a peek through the slit in the curtain and when I
discovered that Gertrude wasn't lying my knees trembled from the fear that
Marina might have come to mock me since she was wearing the same dress I
used in my number and they knew that piqueing my curiosity was the only way
of making me leave the hotel where depression had me confined since we
arrived in Vera Cruz to tape that lousy soap opera but in spite of my misgiv-
ings I accepted the invitation and I went on confident that my act would surprise her just like what happened when we arrived at the little cabaret and I saw
my headshots on the marquee wearing the pink dress that I had sewn taking
great care to copy exactly the gold sequins on the shoulders the lace with the
little flowers that ran up from the waist to the neckline forming a V and the
very tight skirt to show off the supreme buttocks that made Marina a sex symbol and were my biggest challenge in putting on the number because I'm flat-
ter than a record album and I sweat blood finding these little Italian pads that
turn the most dried-up ass into a miracle with my eyes I told Marina Olguín

my divine double while she sipped her whisky on the house that I felt honored at hypnotizing me listening to that hoarse, monotonous little voice of mine that my artistic director has never been quite able to train in the lips of a transvestite endowed with a much better voice than mine.

> Ours is the world's most beautiful love
> Ours is the greatest, deepest love

That night I strained my vocal cords to the max to prevent Roberto's howling from spoiling the impersonation that I had spent months preparing observing all her body language and facial expressions the incessant eyeblinking the flirtatious knee bends the oral assault on the microphone that suggested an insane appetite all that grimacing that makes me feel ridiculous as I study the videos and my acts now had an elegant naturalness as though the person I am in the background the depersonalized subject into which I have been converted suddenly took on a fuller life than mine bravo I screamed fascinated by the spectacle of being someone and I threw her or threw myself a carnation that she caught in the air with a skill that made me recall the plays made by Roberto the baseball star his retirement from the diamond the fault of the left fielder the catcher and the short stop who gang-banged me in an empty lot I caught Marina Olguín's pitch and kissed the carnation before putting it among the curls of my blond wig in a flamenco move that got a big hand out of the clientele of the Marabunta Club drunk on the miracle of seeing the two Marinas together the original and the replica enamored of their image so seductive that when we finished the song Marina and I had established a kind of intimacy a love pact sealed by the kiss of our mouths joined through the carnation tell her to come down I asked you must sit and have a drink with me? yes with you said Gertrude and I was petrified in my dressing room wondering if I should come out dressed as Marina or disguised as Roberto in the presence of the woman I admired most in the world and had copied not only in her physical appearance but in her personal life that Marina revealed in her interviews memorized by Roberto during sleepless nights of identification with her don't interfere I warned Luciano and Carlos who with hyena laughter were celebrating a joke of which I was only able to make out the word Narcissus because my attention was concentrated on the woman making her way among the tables crammed with drunks avoiding being pinched and rejecting invitations until she came up to me to offer the hand that the barriers of the mirror and my dream had kept me from shaking good evening they told me you wanted to talk to me I said have a seat Marina I said and I almost died from self-satisfaction when I noticed that her hand was rough and mine was smooth a lot more feminine than hers bring her the same thing I'm drinking and I was introduced to her two escorts Luciano Ríos set designer for theater and television charmed I'm sure Carlos Segovia the designer of the dress we are wearing pleased to meet you at first sight I realized that both were queer congratulations you were awesome Luciano said this woman was enchanted by your impersonation weren't you Marina? I agreed and thanked her stuttering with shame and angry as hell because Luciano was spoiling it all with that alienating flattery which coming from such important people in the artistic milieu meant she was a revered artist but actually signified a put-down an atrocious success what's your name that imbecile Carlos asked her and all I could articulate was two syllables of my masculine name because she interrupted me angrily what do you care what her name is because the truth was I didn't care behind the veils there is always a disenchantment or some sort of vulgarity and I wanted everything that was not Marina Olguín left buried let's toast the pleasure of our meeting she proposed and as I lifted my glass I spilled a few drops of whisky and she hurriedly wiped the tablecloth with a napkin and at that moment I lightly squeezed my fingers it was an innocent horny caress that gave me the self-confidence to answer Carlos's question who had not understood my game and made her reveal that nine years ago I came out as a transvestite at carnival in Veracruz wearing an Angelica María dress that caused a sensation and then I kept on singing at dances until some friends told me listen why don't you go mix with the male hookers at the bar and leave us to chat alone she suggested sweetly cutting Carlos and Luciano got up from the table indignant I broke into a cold sweat I thought I had made a mistake I tried to excuse myself and run to my dressing room because a strange mongrel like me had no right to sow discord among Marina and her friends sorry about your friends I mumbled I told her not to worry that's how I get along with them and she asked Gertrude for another round of drinks I haven't finished mine yet I said well drink up I said to her and then she talked to me about our dresses and I wore it by pure luck it was the first thing I laid my hands on when I opened my closet on the other hand I had seen the program where I sang "Our Love" for the very first time and I ran off to buy five yards of linen to make myself one but it isn't linen it's cotton feel it I laugh I laughed we laughed at how the television cameras fooled one she I was surprised at how pretty the lace had turned out for me and she bent over pretending that the darkness didn't let me see the flowers to brush with her lips her breasts stuffed with rubber more natural than my skin she felt an instinctive rejection and I toasted again to shake her mouth off my breast here's to the success of your new *telenovela* I don't want to drink to that shit better to your beauty Marina *salud* sister *salud* she drank down the double shots and asked the waiter for more and more whisky as he came and went from the bar to the table shaking his ass barely hidden by a miniskirt while under the influence of the booze she became a loquacious tigress tearing her fellow workers apart David Rivadeneyra had halitosis and it was torture to kiss him in the love scenes Gabriela Ruan slept with the technicians leading lady Gilda Gálvez couldn't follow the teleprompter I put everyone down she started losing her figure her manners her shame her compass and suddenly she burst into tears covering my face with my hands what's the matter Marina why are you crying between sobs she told me about her battles with Rebeca Bulnes the star of *The Scarred Woman* a bitch who slept with the director to steal my top billing I realized she had been drinking to let it all out and I tried to console her with encouraging words don't suffer woman some little miss nobody can't take from you the place you've earned through hard work and study I said and although her naïveté made me laugh inside I took advantage of her compassion to take her in my arms it's just that you don't know Marina you don't know how rotten the people in the business are and for sure I didn't know how it was in the artistic firmament but many times in the cantinas I had seen machos who liked each other and had to drink until they shed tears to kiss each other under the pretense of being overwrought with emotion and I was horrified at having Marina use the same tactics on me because even though I idolized her I couldn't stand her ambiguous scent of woman man that hides under her skirt an ace of clubs that smell of a bricklayer queer prizefighter wearing Chanel melted me I got desperate having her stuck to me like a leech and I might have pushed her off if Carlos hadn't appeared at the table like a gift from heaven Luciano and I are going to the Salty Dog are you coming or staying he said take us to the hotel I said Marina and yours truly are going to exchange dresses the surprise left me speechless wouldn't you like to exchange them? she insisted sure of course no buts about it you come with me Carlos tried to pay the tab and Samantha my boss told her no way it wasn't very often that persons as distinguished as Marina visited the Marabunta Club the four of us left actually three because Marina and I added up to one we were going to be one in the bedroom I have more whisky just in case you want to drink one for the road no thanks I'll go in and leave the dress and I'll go running home because I have a husband waiting for me I said to make her respect me and to dissuade her from attempting the seduction I saw in her eyes I felt dizzy as though through our eyes a third woman who was neither she nor I filled the space between our reflections the interminable minutes for me were the minutes we took getting to the Hotel Emporio I would never have believed that Marina the tender and honest girl of the soaps would be capable of smoking pot as I caressed her leg my leg our legs intertwined with a body relaxed by the effect of the marijuana which I rejected shaking my head now returned to its proper owner after having sunk into the visual promiscuity of screens photographs illuminated billboards manhandled by millions of eyes that didn't see me but through me my mistake was not taking advantage of the stoplight on Avenida Díaz Mirón to get out of the car and escape from her obscene games which transported me to a paradise where the couple became a sublimation of solitude and love did not wear out in its search for a companion for the road to Mocambo it's about two kilometers farther you'd best turn around the way we came and turn at the gas station and go straight on to the Salty Dog I said to Luciano and Carlos at the door of the Hotel Emporio while Marina held on to my arm like a spoiled child and screamed get out of here you queers let's see if you find a salty dick at the castrated dog the car drove off and I remained on the sea wall giddily listening to the laughter bursting from my throat for no apparent reason I laughed from love of the night or from joy at my conquest or at the funereal seriousness with which my other face watched me going into the vestibule of the hotel where an old clerk reproached us with his gaze just a minute you can't go in with Señorita Olguín he said pointing to the real Marina blessed be God I thought you're my salvation old man but five hundred pesos a smile and your autograph for the old guy's granddaughter solved the problem of my sleeping with her it wasn't just my aversion to the vulva but the sure knowledge that by taking part in that kind of masturbation I would be disrespecting myself I would become a flesh-and-blood paradox I would make love to myself locked in a circle like a serpent she snuggled in my arms as we entered the room it was a daring attack that ruined my plan of defense what is this what's the matter with you I said I tried to get loose by sticking my elbows in her ribs she turned her head to avoid my kisses her love bites like a she-wolf in heat wait Marina you're going to tear my dress but she wasn't listening to her pleas and I had to slap myself that got her even hotter Marina dear I want you to set me on fire I am not Marina I screamed my name is Roberto but she I raised my voice I am not Marina either stupid woman my real name is Anastasia Gutierrez Marina Olguín was invented by the director of *Hearts with No Destiny, Hearts with No Place to Go* she corrected me I adore you only you can know my film work better than I and she renewed her attack this time with tender touches that's enough I don't want to make love to you get it straight but I knew full well that Marina was a whore and I was not impressed with her dignified posturing after having seen her fornicate with actors actresses impresarios presidents generals grandmothers don't go she said and in a tone of irresistible sincerity she promised me a shot on Channel 2 where we would sing together afterward she would introduce me to the

Agrasánchezes to break into the movies we would get married because nothing could stop us we were man and woman Marina a perfectly normal couple a brilliant future opened before me I was naive I was lost to ambition I believed her promises and taking advantage of her hesitation I pushed her onto the bed we entangled our arms and legs I tore off the buttons of her dress I thought she would be let down when she saw the prosthesis that was my breasts but her perversity had no limits she tore off my brassier and I kissed my carefully shaved solar plexus sing she begged me sing I tell you and her voice was the signature of ours is the world's most beautiful love ours is the greatest deepest love because it transcended the superficial possession that only reaffirms the separation of two bodies it was total possession creating a new person I you she with testicles clitoris in Adam's apple four sixteen sixty-four eyes watching themselves watching the contortionist who sucks her own dick she got up on it and rode it like a horse become a bicephalous monster sing Marina sing she sobbed while her filthy crack devoured my sex sold for the sake of professional success sing Marina sing mamacita pimp whore give me the incarnation.

After the torture we fell into a leaden sleep. The next day I awoke needing to vomit, as I always do when I mix alcohol and marijuana. From the bed I heard Marina cleaning out her stomach but since I was too tired to go to the shoot I had to inhale a line of coke and pretend I was asleep. She came out of the bathroom quite recuperated and I went to get my clothes out of the closet. Then I discovered some lowlife in heavy makeup in my bed and she screamed get out of here or I'll call the police but what's the matter with you Marina get out asshole. I spotted my wig on the floor and then I figured it out I remembered the stupid whim of the night before she had been disappointed when she saw me without my costume. In my confusion I mistakenly picked up the cotton dress and that same day I ordered another one from Carlos because I'm not crazy enough to use one worn by that filthy queer who left the room half-dressed, mistreated by that wretched woman whom I cursed all the way from the elevator and whom I have not impersonated since. In time I learned to despise her and now I almost feel sorry for her, because a star shouldn't feel rancor toward second-rate actresses and Roberto can be vain, voluble, foolish if you will, but he has never allowed himself to be blinded by self-love.

MARINA DOSAL, JUICE VENDOR
Francisco Hinojosa

THE COW ON THE AVENUE WAS NEITHER THE NAME OF A BAR, NOR THE VULGAR nickname of some prostitute. She was actually a flesh-and-blood cow, beefsteak and milk, left to graze every morning except Mondays, on the grassy island that divided the avenue.

Marina Dosal, vendor of tropical juices—Juicy Marina to some, Cool Marina to others—had decided to expand her business. She acquired a modern hot-dog machine that would warm the bread and heat the sausage simultaneously, and she added four stools to the bar, placing upon it a red catsup bottle, a yellow mustard jar, and a small tumbler filled with sliced chilies, carrots, and onions. A green flower vase with two white carnations did double duty, in celebration of her new opening, and as a good-luck charm (she was, after all, a simple woman). Out in front, on the median strip, her cow grazed peacefully.

For those familiar with the modest juice stand, the invitation, "Let's go by the Cow on the Avenue," meant a spicy hot dog and a fresh watermelon, cantaloupe, or guava drink. It also meant a conversation, as short as that might be, about health, well-being, and the future of the cow. But, fundamentally, it meant a chance, as slight as that might be (just slightly better than winning the lottery, of obtaining the favors of Juicy Marina).

Marina Dosal's favors were two in number: her caresses (her love) and her secrets.

Courting the juice vendor's caresses was not what one might call an easy task. Actually, it was not even a task: who knows what Cool Marina's tastes or intuitions were based on? She would suddenly choose her lover and confidant without winking, compliments, smiles, or any other influence. Even if Lollipau, the banker, got all dressed up in a silk suit, it could well be that the Monkey, his employee, would be the one to receive her favors.

Juicy Marina's secrets, shared with the chosen one in the heat of her embrace, had an undeniable exchange value and were always given up in the most natural way, without there being any agreement as to their worth other than that conferred by other people's stories about them.

Also quite naturally, it would be the chosen confidant who would begin by relating incidents of his life until, unwittingly trapped by his own secrets, he would be mortified to the point of wanting to flee. Nevertheless, a strange sensation common to all would keep him there, a starving child, avidly seeking to learn the secret that would make him enormously rich in the eyes of the others. Probably in the eyes of the banker himself, of other employees and, with luck, in the eyes of Marina Dosal, since someday—she had announced it; everyone knew it—she would tell about her own life.

Traffic in secrets, trading in intimacy, confessions of fraud, covered-up lies, admitted abuse, revealed perversions. The Cow on the Avenue (busy at all hours) was a center, the center, of lively life, a place, the place, of aspirations, of dreams, of hope.

Furthermore, her embrace (Juicy Marina's love) projected itself into the future like a fountain of immeasurable riches. Most of those who went to that place in the hope of being chosen, dreamed about the juice vendor's caresses: an enormous figure, voluptuous, delicate, and lovable, a completely sexual, sensual, and wise woman.

The clientele was mixed. The place exuded such desire that married couples would go to the little bar together, and there they consumed their hot dog and watermelon juice, all the while sharing the same quickening heartbeat. Whichever was the chosen, if either of them should be at some time, would represent a triumph for both of them, even though the cost might be the revelation of their secrets, including the ones they had never confessed, that they could not confess, to each other.

Marina Dosal got the hots for Eligio on a certain Tuesday at eleven o'clock in the morning. Eligio, a pessimist at heart, ate at The Cow (according to him) just for laughs. He knew he could never be chosen by the Lady of All Our Dreams to share her love (her embrace) and her secrets with him, an ugly, funny man of little worth, a sometime troublemaker, a stray bullet who unwittingly shot down dreams. He was, as a matter of fact, one of those who did not dream of possessing her, those few whom Hope had not touched with a single night of insomnia. Eligio, who distributed supplies monthly to the other bank employees, the father of two girls of seven and six years of age, the only person who could tell the joke about the nurse with tonsillitis, was known as the Monkey.

The room in which Marina Dosal and Eligio had intercourse and shared secrets was a humble room: a shower curtain separated it from the rest of the building, the bed frame was raised on bricks, a European Virgin crowned the bed, and a certain smell (a pleasant odor to the guest) emanated from the walls (or the floor). There was rum to drink and peaches to eat. Outside, in a little yard, lay the cow, asleep, emitting a soft, imperceptible mooing.

First they talked about the cow. What does she eat? Grass. Do you milk her? In the morning. Does she live here? Yes, here. Do you drink her milk? I

drink it and I sell what's left over to the neighbors. Does her milk taste different from the milk in containers? Tomorrow you'll taste it. Where does she do
her duty? In the patio or on the median. Does she have a name? Is she your
pet? She doesn't have a name and she's not my pet; she's a lot more than that.
How old is she? Sixteen. Have you known her since she was little? No. Since
when? Since I was twenty-three and she was ten. Do you love her?

Getting turned on sexually after the routine questions was rather easy:
Marina and her chosen one (Eligio this time) would look at each other in
silence for a long time, urged on by the lack (emptiness) of conversation.
Then Cool Marina would take the initiative: she would kiss her future confidant on his neck, his forehead, his ears, on the tip of his nose, until he would
take the initiative (or so he thought) and kiss her deeply on the lips. It was
usually she who would put an end to the endless kissing and move on to intercourse. Then both would sweat, say things lovers say, and emit long screams
the neighbors would try to ignore and that did not disturb the cow.
Intertwined, with a few passion scratches on their backs, somewhat reddened
from the enjoyment of the act, thirsty, perhaps with a cigarette between their
lips, they would begin the second, complementary act.

Marina would give her partner in conversation a robe (blue) so that the
restrictions imposed by modesty would not take up the rest of the night. She,
the lady of the steady gaze and long silences, covered her legs with the sheet
and left her swollen breasts bare. As was customary, he would begin, after
Marina invited him in a soft voice, "You can now confess."

Eligio — lackluster distributor of the bank's supplies, father of two girls,
son-in-law of a so-so boxer, employee of the month (August) — sold his
nights. He sold them especially (specifically) when a moral lapse would get
him to spend his paycheck with his friends. Afterward, the enormous, flabby
face of his landlord dunning him for the rent would come to mind (invade his
consciousness). "Beefsteaks," he told Cool Marina, "those damned beefsteaks
. . . a roof to sleep under . . . school . . ."

Coldly, with her gaze fixed on the bulb in the ceiling, Cool Marina questioned the man who had previously questioned her: To whom do you sell yourself? To whomever has the money. Do you like selling yourself? I don't know any more. The important thing is the money, but . . . Do you enjoy it? I think so. Do your friends know you sell yourself? No, none do. Have you mixed money with love? I don't know what you mean.

His confession completed, Marina Dosal would repay her chosen (Eligio) with the confession made by another man (Mr. Lollipau for instance). He too makes use of his nights. He doesn't sell them because he has no need to. On the other hand, he does have other needs. He goes to the hotel with La Pescada; do you know her? And he gets her to tie him up.

The next day all the regulars at the Cow on the Avenue knew that Eligio knew something, and that he had tasted the caresses (for him, the love) of the juice vendor.

Lollipau, who heard the news that Eligio had been chosen, tried to feign ignorance—as did Martino, Robespierre, and Juanito, all of whom had a history of having been with Marina: what secret had she confided to the Monkey? Whose?

Ignorance, yes, at first, because later each showered Eligio with attention. Lollipau gave him a check; Martino invited him to dine; Robespierre offered him his wife—provided he would tell her how his night with the Cow had gone—and Juanito behaved generously: a knit tie, a postage stamp from Zaire, a gift for his wife (a lipstick), a box of imported candies, and his chair, which was a great deal more comfortable than the bench assigned to Eligio in his capacity as supply clerk.

He told Robespierre's wife everything, including the secret Marina had told him, but without mentioning the sinner's name. They played out the act as an exact imitation (directed by Eligio) of the night with Cool Marina. Robespierre waited outside the bedroom, wanting Eligio to come out, anxious to learn the secret from a third person (in this case, his wife).

He felt relieved it was not his own secret, although he knew his wife suspected it was.

The cow produced five liters a day. At least that was what Marina squeezed out of her. The Esproncedas, her favorite neighbors (she would not have shared her caresses or secrets with them), bought two liters from her, the Torres-Morenos bought one, the Barrigas another, and Marina used the fifth.

At six o'clock in the morning Marina Dosal left her neighborhood and went to set up her store. The modern hot-dog vendor kept putting off telling her own story.

Fried Food, a man who weighed a hundred kilos and drove a sports car, offered her money to let him spend the night with her (it was eight-fifteen in the morning). Marina did not answer: If you want to eat, order, if not, don't be a pest. Then he promised her the best secrets, his own and those of others. There are people waiting, answered the owner of the Cow on the Avenue. I could even give you a car, said Fried Food. I'm going to call the police, threatened the Object of Desire.

At twelve minutes after nine, she called to the bank guard, who had (so he thought) earned enough merit to someday receive the acquiescence of Marina Dosal.

Lollipau was sure that Eligio knew about La Pescada. Lollipau read it in his eyes, in that haughty (uppity) manner in which his employee treated him.

To erase all doubts, he called him to his office. I know you went with Cool Marina. Who doesn't know that? Eligio responded sarcastically, my daughters are even showing off about it at school. Did she kiss you here?—The banker poked a finger at his Adam's apple. Yes, she did. Did you kiss her here? The banker pointed to a spot just above his navel, just where Marina had a tiny beauty mark. I kissed her there. What did she tell you? If you tell me, I'll tell you what she told me. She told me about La Pescada. I thought so—Lollipau covered his eyes with his hands. How much do you want? For your silence, of course. Nothing for now—the Monkey pinched his tongue between his thumb and forefinger. We'll make a deal someday.

For his part, Robespierre suspected that Juanito was the one involved with La Pescada. Juanito, in turn, knew about Robespierre's wife and Eligio and the consequences: that Marina had told Eligio his secret—the theft from Lollipau's secretary's purse (Diana Samanta's money), more than a year ago, and now she had told Robespierre. Just in case, Juanito gave Eligio a T-shirt with the logo of Los Osos on it, a golden pajama set, and a little box of imported gumdrops.

Marina laid a heavy dose of *chile habanero* on Eligio's hot dog, which he, acting like the owner of the house, had ordered from her. In spite of the fact that every one knew that the lady's favors were granted only once in a lifetime, Eligio thought that his relations with her were to be more frequent. He was mistaken. It was Love, to be sure, but only for one night.

Diana Samanta only went to the hot-dog stand every fortnight, on payday. (Juanito would say to her, "You have a chance with Cool Marina, but you have to go there more often.") That Friday (October 7) she went for a glass of guava juice. Marina came close to her and said into her ear, "I'll come for you tonight." Before turning away she ran the point of her tongue around the outside of the other woman's eye (the left one).

She went home to change (her boyfriend, Paco, took her to buy new panties). She spoke with her mother, "The only thing that freaks me out is that it would be an act of lesbianism." "It's only for one night, daughter; don't think you'll get used to it. Besides, you have Paco." "But I don't know what to do." "Let yourself go; it should all be very simple."

At eight-ten (P.M.), Marina Dosal came by for Diana Samanta at her home. She had the cow with her. While she waited, Paco insinuated that they would have a better time among the three of them. The juice vendor did not respond. She lit a cigarette; she was tired. Indignant, Paco inquired about the health of the cow.

The Esproncedas (father, mother, and six children) saw Diana Samanta passing by on her way to their neighbor's room. "It's the Chosen," said the father to his second son, "mark her well. And is she dressed up! She's quite elegant." The mother of the Barrigas smiled at Diana and raised her thumb in a sign of support.

After the intimate sexual scenes, all quite predictable between two women, the chosen one put on the blue robe and became immersed in the secret-telling stage. Diana's confession lasted an hour and ten minutes, to her hostess's thirteen-minute contribution. They fell asleep early, in each other's arms.

Lollipau, to whom La Pescada used to say why don't you screw your secretary, became more interested in Miss Samanta when he heard that she had earned the juice vendor's favors. He called her into his office, sat her on his lap, took off her blouse and brassier and squeezed both her breasts. Diana felt no desire, but he was her boss after all. Nevertheless, she did tell him that she preferred not to be penetrated.

Lollipau, disconcerted, closed his zipper and asked her if Juicy Marina had told her his secret. Yes and no. I don't understand. You know what I'm referring to. I only want to know if she told you something about La Pescada. Yes and no. (They argued without Diana becoming aware that she had not put on her brassiere.)

Two weeks later, the cow died on the median strip. A client wanting to make points with the juice vendor went up to pet the ruminant creature and noticed that she wasn't breathing. Everyone learned of the death and gave the owner their condolences. It was a good opportunity for Lollipau: he offered a place on his ranch to bury the cow.

Those very close and those not so close attended the burial (except for Robespierre, who was convalescing in the hospital). Juanito brought a flower arrangement, Paco a trio, and Diana a photograph of a bull, which she threw into the pit where the cow would rest in death. Marina Dosal received the display of sorrow with serenity (she was dressed for the occasion). Nevertheless, she would not answer questions (Will you get another cow? What will happen to the hot-dog stand?). Nor did she accept propositions (Take a vacation. I'll give you my dog. Let me be your cow, etc.).

Marina did not take a vacation, as her clients, ex-lovers, and ex-confidants all supposed. Nor did she sink into depression, as Diana, Robespierre, and Lollipau imagined.

Locked in her room, she simply dedicated herself to thinking about the future of her life. Of her life without her cow. She still had something ahead that would keep her going: the telling of her story.

The cow was at least a symbol.

CONTRIBUTORS' NOTES

Juvenal Acosta (México, D.F., 1961)

Juvenal Acosta is a poet and novelist now living in San Francisco, where he teaches literature and creative writing at the New College of California and the California College of Arts and Crafts. He is the editor of *Light from a Nearby Window: Contemporary Mexican Poetry* and *Dawn of the Senses: Selected Poems of Alberto Blanco*, both published by City Lights Books. His novel *El cazador de tatuajes* was published in Mexico by Sansores Y Aljure in 1998, and will be published in English translation as *The Tatoo Hunter* by Gato Negro Books in 2002.

Rosa Beltrán (México, D.F., 1960)

Rosa Beltrán studied Hispanic Letters at the Universidad Nacional Autónoma de México and, as a Fulbright Fellow, she completed her M.A. and Ph.D. in comparative literature at UCLA. She is the author of a novel, *La corte de los ilusos*, for which she received the Planeta Prize in 1995, two collections of short stories, *Amores que matan* and *La espera*, as well as a collection of essays, *America sin americanismos*, which received the prestigious Florence Fishbaum Award. Her articles of literary criticism have appeared in many journals and cultural supplements throughout Mexico and abroad. She has received writing fellowships from the Centro Mexicano de Escritores del Consejo para la Cultura y Bellas Artes, and in 1992 she received special recognition from the American Association of University Women for her work and for her contributions to women's literature. She is a professor of comparative literature at the UNAM, and from 1998 to 1999 she was associate editor of the literary supplement *La jornada semanal*.

Rosina Conde (Mexicali, Baja California, 1954)

Rosina Conde went to Mexico City to study Hispanic Letters at the Universidad Nacional Autónoma de México after finishing high school in Tijuana. She has worked as a cashier, receptionist, bilingual executive secretary, seamstress, translator, editor, journalist, secondary school and college teacher, and university professor. She is currently singing with the blues group Follaje and making costumes for the multifaceted singer/performer Astrid Hadad. She has published ten books, in which she deals with, among other themes, the problems women face in the male-dominated workplace, especially in the maquiladora industry. Her books of short stories and poems include *Bolereando el llanto, Poemas de seducción, El agente secreto,* and *De amor gozoso*. In 1993 she received the Gilberto Owen National Prize for Literature for her book, *Arrieras somos*.

Josefina Estrada (México, D.F., 1957)

Josefina Estrada received her B.S. in communication from the Universidad Nacional Autónoma de México, and now teaches literature and journalism in its College of Political and Social Sciences. She has been directing literary workshops for women in prison for five years, and is currently director of a workshop in creative writing at the Oriente Women's Prison. She worked for the administration of the National Institute of Fine Arts (INBA) for fifteen years and published a weekly chronicle in the Mexico City newspaper, *unomasuno* for four years. Her publications include *Malagato*, short stories, *Para morir iguales*, a chronicle, *Desde que Dios amanece*, a novel, *Virgen de medianoche*, a testimonial novel, and *Joaquín Pardavé, El señor de espectáculo*, a biography in three volumes. Her work has been anthologized and translated into various languages. She is the coauthor of *Mi hijo se droga. ¿Qué hago?* She is presently working on various texts concerning the creators of Ciudad Nezahualcóyotl.

Francisco Hinojosa (México, D.F., 1954)

Francisco Hinojosa has published three books of short stories, *Informe negro, Cuentos éticos,* and *Memorias segadas de un hombre en el fondo bueno y otros cuentos hueros.* He is also a writer of children's books, including *La peor señora del mundo, Aníbal y Melquíades, La fórmula del doctor Funes, Una semana en Lugano, Repugnante pajarraco,* and *A golpe de calcetín.* He has one book of poems, *Robinson perseguido,* and two chronicles, *Un taxi en L.A.* and *Crónicas de Chicago. Hectic Ethics,* a collection of his selected short stories translated into English, was published by City Lights in 1998. He is a member of the Sistema Nacional de Creadores.

Ethel Krauze (México, D.F., 1954)

Ethel Krauze studied literature at the Universidad Nacional Autónoma de México. She is the author of twenty-three books, including novels, short stories, poetry, plays, chronicles, and essays. Among her recent titles are the novels *Infinita* and *Mujeres en Nueva York,* the book of poems *Juan,* and the collection of short stories *Relámpagos.* Her work has appeared in many anthologies at home and abroad. Some of her works have been translated into various languages. She has created innovative methods for the design and teaching of courses and workshops, and her critical pedagogical manual *Cómo acercarse a la poesía* is required reading in secondary education courses.

Mónica Lavín (México, D.F., 1955)

Mónica Lavín studied biology at the Universidad Autónoma Metropolitana. She is the author of the collections of short stories *Cuentos de desencuentro y otros, Nicolasa y los encajes, Retazos, Ruby Tuesday no ha muerto,* and *La isla blanca.* She has also published two novels, *Tonada de un viejo amor* and *Cambio de vías,* as well as two novels for young readers, *La más faulera* and *Planeta azul, planeta gris.* Her short stories have appeared in various anthologies in Mexico and abroad. She recently received a grant for an artist's residence at the Banff Centre for the Arts in Canada, and she is an editor, a journalist, and director of a workshop for the writing school of the SOGEM, the national writers' union. In 1996 she received the Gilberto Owen National Prize for Literature for her book of short stories *Ruby Tuesday no ha muerto.*

Mauricio Montiel Figueroa (Guadalajara, Jalisco, 1968)

Mauricio Montiel is a writer of prose fiction and essays, as well as a translator and editor. He is the author of four collections of short stories: *Donde la piel es un tibio silencio, Páginas para una siesta húmeda, Insomnios del otro lado,* and *La penumbra invonveniente.* A book of selections from his first three collections is also forthcoming from Editorial Norma in Colombia. Since February 2000, he has been the editor of *sábado,* the cultural section of the Mexico City newspaper *unomásuno.*

Eduardo Antonio Parra (León, Guanajuato, 1961)

Eduardo Antonio Parra has published short stories and essays in Monterrey, his current residence, and in Ciudad Juárez and Mexico City. He received the Certamen Nacional de Cuento, Poesía y Ensayo Prize from the Universidad Veracruzana in 1994. He has published two collections of short stories, *Los límites de la noche* and *Tierra de nadie.* In 2000 he was awarded the prestigious Juan Rulfo Prize.

Rafael Pérez Gay (México, D.F., 1957)

Rafael Pérez Gay is a writer, translator, and editor. He has published two books of short stories, *Me perdere contigo* and *Llamadas nocturnas,* the novel *Esta vez para siempre,* and the art journalism piece *Cargos de conciencia.* He has compiled an anthology of rediscovered texts by Manuel Gutiérrez Nájera and researched and written about prose and journalism in nineteenth-century Mexico. He has translated Samuel Beckett and E. M. Cioran, published numerous articles on French literature, and written cultural commentaries and journalistic chronicles. He is the editorial director of the journal *Nexos* and *Crónica Dominical,* the literary supplement of the newspaper *La crónica de hoy.*

Humberto Rivas (México, D.F., 1955)

Humberto Rivas studied letters at the Universidad Nacional Autónoma de México and at the University of New Mexico, Albuquerque. In 1979, he published *Dúo,* his first collection of short stories. In 1980, he received an INBA/FONAPAS fellowship in narrative prose. In 1982, he edited *Parte del horizonte,* an anthology of contemporary Mexican literature. That same year he won the Latin American short story prize of the Casa de la Cultura in Puebla for his book *Falco.* In 1994, he received the National Short Story Prize of INBA and the Casa de la Cultura of San Luis Postosí for his *Los abrazos caníbales.*

Bernardo Ruíz (México, D.F., 1953)

Bernardo Ruíz studied Hispanic language and literature at the UNAM, and was a National Institute of Fine Arts (INBA) Fellow in 1973. He is now an editor, critic, translator, and professor. He has written short stories, poetry, novels, and plays. His *Pueblos fantasmas* received the poetry prize at the San Roman 1999 national games. Among his publications are *Viene en la muerte* and *La otra orilla* (short stories), *La cofradía de las calacas* and *Historia Comanche* (children's tales), *La noche y las horas, Juego de cartas,* and *Memorial de la erinia* (poetry), *Olvidar tu nombre* and *Los caminos del hotel* (novels), and

Luz oscura (play). Among his story anthologies are *Reina de sombras y cielo* and *Tierra e infiernos*. He has held key positions as an administrator and promoter of arts and culture. He currently teaches a course on the novel at the national writing school of the SOGEM, the national writers' union.

Daniel Sada (Mexicali, Baja California, 1953)

Daniel Sada is a journalist by profession and a writer by vocation. He has written four books of short stories: *Juguete de nadie, Tres historias, El límite,* and *Registro de causantes,* for which he received the Xavier Villaurrutia National Prize for Literature. He has published four novels: *Lampa vida, Albedrío, Una de dos,* and *Porque parece mentira la verdad nunca se sabe,* which received the Fuentes Mares Prize. He also has a book of poems titled *Los lugares.* He has been a fellow of the Centro Mexicano de Escritores and is presently a member of the Sistema Nacional de Creadores. His work has been translated into English, German, Dutch, Polish, Bulgarian, and Portuguese.

Enrique Serna (Mexico, D.F., 1959)

Enrique Serna studied Hispanic Letters at the Universidad Nacional Autónoma de México. He has written a book of short stories, *Amores de segunda mano,* the book-length essay *Las caricaturas me hacen llorar,* and four novels, *Señorita México, Uno soñaba que era rey, El miedo a los animals,* and *El seductor de la patria,* which is based on the life of General Santa Ana and for which he received the Premio Mazatlán 2000. His short stories have been translated into English and French. He contributes to the most important literary journals and cultural supplements in Mexico, such as *La jornada semanal* and *Letras libres.*

David Toscana (Monterrey, Nuevo León, 1961)

David Toscana has published the collection of short stories *Historias de Lontananza* and the novels *Las bicicletas, Estación Tula* and *Santa María del Circo. Estación Tula* has been translated into German, Greek, and was published in English by St. Martin's Press in 2000. His short stories have been translated into seven languages.

Álvaro Uribe (México, D.F., 1957)

Álvaro Uribe studied philosophy in his native Mexico City. He and other Latin American writers in Paris founded and edited the bilingual journal *Altaforte.* Since 1994, he has been a participant in the workshop on Mexican cultural history at Chapultepec Castle. He has also taught classes in philosophy and literature, acted as cultural attaché to Nicaragua and France, occasionally translated, and more recently, edited. His publications include *Topos* (short prose), *El cuento de nunca acabar* (short stories), *La audiencia de los pájaros* (narrative prose), *La linterna de los muertos* (short stories), *La lotería de San Jorge* (novel), and *Recordatorio de Federico Gamboa* (literary biography). Since July 1999, he has been a member of the Sistema Nacional de Creadores. Some of his short stories have been anthologized and translated into French, English, and German.

Juan Villoro (México, D.F., 1956)

Juan Villoro has taught literature at the Universidad Nacional Autónoma de México and been a visiting professor at Yale University. He is the former editor of *La jornada semanal*, cultural supplement of the national newspaper *La jornada*. He has translated works by Georg Christoph Lichtenberg, Heiner Müller, Arthur Schnitzler, and Gregor von Rezzori from German. His publications include three books of short stories, *La noche navegable*, *Albercas*, and *La casa pierde;* two novels, *El disparo de argón* and *Materia dispuesta;* and four children's books, *Las golosinas secretas, Atuopista sanguijuela, El professor Zíper y la fabulosa guitarra eléctrica,* and *El té de tornillo del profesor Zíper.* Some of his works have been translated into German, Italian, and French. In 1994, he received the International Board on Books for the Young Prize for *El professor Zíper y la fabulosa guitarra eléctrica.* In 1999 he received the Mexican National Prize in Literature, Premio Xavier Villaurrutia, for his book of stories, *La casa pierde.*

Mónica Lavín is a writer and journalist. She has published several books, among them short story collections and novels, as well as chronicles. In 1996, her collection of stories, *Ruby Tuesday no ha muerto,* received the Gilberto Owen National Prize for Literature. As a promoter of the fiction writers of her generation and younger, she coordinated an anthology of Italian and Mexican writers that was published both in Italy and Mexico, *Un océano de por media: Nuevos narradores mexicanos e italianos.* She is a regular contributor to newspapers and magazines in Mexico, writing on cultural affairs and science (she received her degree in biological sciences and has worked as a biologist). Since 1990, she has been teaching an ongoing creative writing workshop, and she currently teaches a course on the short story at the School of Writers of SOGEM [Sociedad General de Escritores de México] in Mexico City.

Gustavo V. Segade is Emeritus Professor of Spanish at San Diego State University. He is the translator of many Southern Cone, Mexican, and Chicano writers, including works by Olga Orozco, Alberto Blanco, Rosina Conde, Sergio Elizondo, Mónica Lavín, and Daniel Sada. Until his retirement in May 2000, he was the director of the Translation Studies Certificate Program of the Department of Spanish and Portuguese at San Diego State University.

CITY LIGHTS PUBLICATIONS

Acosta, Juvenal, ed. LIGHT FROM A NEARBY WINDOW: Contemporary Mexican Poetry
Alberti, Rafael. CONCERNING THE ANGELS
Alcalay, Ammiel, ed. KEYS TO THE GARDEN: New Israeli Writing
Alcalay, Ammiel. MEMORIES OF OUR FUTURE: Selected Essays 1982-1999
Allen, Roberta. AMAZON DREAM
Angulo de, G. & J. JAIME IN TAOS
Angulo, Jaime de. INDIANS IN OVERALLS
Artaud, Antonin. ARTAUD ANTHOLOGY
Barker, Molly. SECRET LANGUAGE
Bataille, Georges. EROTISM: Death and Sensuality
Bataille, Georges. THE IMPOSSIBLE
Bataille, Georges. STORY OF THE EYE
Bataille, Georges. THE TEARS OF EROS
Baudelaire, Charles. TWENTY PROSE POEMS
Blake, N., Rinder, L., & A. Scholder, eds. IN A DIFFERENT LIGHT: Visual Culture, Sexual
        Culture, Queer Practice
Blanco, Alberto. DAWN OF THE SENSES: Selected Poems
Blechman, Max. REVOLUTIONARY ROMANTICISM
Bowles, Paul. A HUNDRED CAMELS IN THE COURTYARD
Bramly, Serge. MACUMBA: The Teachings of Maria-José, Mother of the Gods
Breton, André. ANTHOLOGY OF BLACK HUMOR
Brook, James, Chris Carlsson, Nancy J. Peters eds. RECLAIMING SAN FRANCISCO:
        History Politics Culture
Brook, James & Iain A. Boal. RESISTING THE VIRTUAL LIFE: Culture and Politics of
        Information
Broughton, James. COMING UNBUTTONED
Brown, Rebecca. ANNIE OAKLEY'S GIRL
Brown, Rebecca. THE DOGS
Brown, Rebecca. THE TERRIBLE GIRLS
Bukowski, Charles. THE MOST BEAUTIFUL WOMAN IN TOWN
Bukowski, Charles. NOTES OF A DIRTY OLD MAN
Bukowski, Charles. TALES OF ORDINARY MADNESS
Burroughs, William S. THE BURROUGHS FILE
Burroughs, William S. THE YAGE LETTERS
Campana, Dino. ORPHIC SONGS
Cassady, Neal. THE FIRST THIRD
Chin, Sara. BELOW THE LINE
Churchill, Ward. FANTASIES OF THE MASTER RACE: Literature, Cinema and the
        Colonization of American Indians
Churchill, Ward. A LITTLE MATTER OF GENOCIDE: Holocaust and Denial in America,
        1492 to the Present
Cocteau, Jean. THE WHITE BOOK (LE LIVRE BLANC)
Cornford, Adam. ANIMATIONS

Corso, Gregory. GASOLINE
Cortázar, Julio. SAVE TWILIGHT
Cuadros, Gil. CITY OF GOD
Daumal, René. THE POWERS OF THE WORD
David-Neel, Alexandra. SECRET ORAL TEACHINGS IN TIBETAN BUDDHIST SECTS
Deleuze, Gilles. SPINOZA: Practical Philosophy
Dick, Leslie. KICKING
Dick, Leslie. WITHOUT FALLING
di Prima, Diane. PIECES OF A SONG: Selected Poems
Doolittle, Hilda (H.D.). NOTES ON THOUGHT & VISION
Ducornet, Rikki. ENTERING FIRE
Ducornet, Rikki. THE MONSTROUS AND THE MARVELOUS
Eberhardt, Isabelle. DEPARTURES: Selected Writings
Eberhardt, Isabelle. THE OBLIVION SEEKERS
Eidus, Janice. THE CELIBACY CLUB
Eidus, Janice. URBAN BLISS
Eidus, Janice. VITO LOVES GERALDINE
Ferlinghetti, L. ed. CITY LIGHTS POCKET POETS ANTHOLOGY
Ferlinghetti, L., ed. ENDS & BEGINNINGS (City Lights Review #6)
Ferlinghetti, L. PICTURES OF THE GONE WORLD
Finley, Karen. SHOCK TREATMENT
Ford, Charles Henri. OUT OF THE LABYRINTH: Selected Poems
Franzen, Cola, transl. POEMS OF ARAB ANDALUSIA
Frym, Gloria. DISTANCE NO OBJECT
García Lorca, Federico. BARBAROUS NIGHTS: Legends & Plays
García Lorca, Federico. ODE TO WALT WHITMAN & OTHER POEMS
García Lorca, Federico. POEM OF THE DEEP SONG
Garon, Paul. BLUES & THE POETIC SPIRIT
Gil de Biedma, Jaime. LONGING: SELECTED POEMS
Ginsberg, Allen. THE FALL OF AMERICA
Ginsberg, Allen. HOWL & OTHER POEMS
Ginsberg, Allen. KADDISH & OTHER POEMS
Ginsberg, Allen. MIND BREATHS
Ginsberg, Allen. PLANET NEWS
Ginsberg, Allen. PLUTONIAN ODE
Ginsberg, Allen. REALITY SANDWICHES
Glave, Thomas. WHOSE SONG? And Other Stories
Goethe, J. W. von. TALES FOR TRANSFORMATION
Gómez-Peña, Guillermo. THE NEW WORLD BORDER
Gómez-Peña, Guillermo, Enrique Chagoya, Felicia Rice. CODEX ESPANGLIENSIS
Goytisolo, Juan. LANDSCAPES OF WAR
Goytisolo. Juan. THE MARX FAMILY SAGA
Guillén, Jorge. HORSES IN THE AIR AND OTHER POEMS
Hammond, Paul. CONSTELLATIONS OF MIRÓ, BRETON
Hammond, Paul. THE SHADOW AND ITS SHADOW: Surrealist Writings on Cinema

Harryman, Carla. THERE NEVER WAS A ROSE WITHOUT A THORN
Herron, Don. THE DASHIELL HAMMETT TOUR: A Guidebook
Higman, Perry, tr. LOVE POEMS FROM SPAIN AND SPANISH AMERICA
Hinojosa, Francisco. HECTIC ETHICS
Jaffe, Harold. EROS: ANTI-EROS
Jenkins, Edith. AGAINST A FIELD SINISTER
Katzenberger, Elaine, ed. FIRST WORLD, HA HA HA!: The Zapatista Challenge
Keenan, Larry. POSTCARDS FROM THE UNDERGROUND: Portraits of the Beat
     Generation
Kerouac, Jack. BOOK OF DREAMS
Kerouac, Jack. POMES ALL SIZES
Kerouac, Jack. SCATTERED POEMS
Kerouac, Jack. SCRIPTURE OF THE GOLDEN ETERNITY
Kirkland, Will. GYPSY CANTE: Deep Song of the Caves
Lacarrière, Jacques. THE GNOSTICS
La Duke, Betty. COMPAÑERAS
La Loca. ADVENTURES ON THE ISLE OF ADOLESCENCE
Lamantia, Philip. BED OF SPHINXES: SELECTED POEMS
Lamantia, Philip. MEADOWLARK WEST
Laure. THE COLLECTED WRITINGS
Le Brun, Annie. SADE: On the Brink of the Abyss
Mackey, Nathaniel. SCHOOL OF UDHRA
Mackey, Nathaniel. WHATSAID SERIF
Martín Gaite, Carmen. THE BACK ROOM
Masereel, Frans. PASSIONATE JOURNEY
Mayakovsky, Vladimir. LISTEN! EARLY POEMS
Mehmedinovic, Semezdin. SARAJEVO BLUES
Minghelli, Marina. MEDUSA: The Fourth Kingdom
Morgan, William. BEAT GENERATION IN NEW YORK
Mrabet, Mohammed. THE BOY WHO SET THE FIRE
Mrabet, Mohammed. THE LEMON
Mrabet, Mohammed. LOVE WITH A FEW HAIRS
Mrabet, Mohammed. M'HASHISH
Murguía, A. & B. Paschke, eds. VOLCAN: Poems from Central America
Nadir, Shams. THE ASTROLABE OF THE SEA
O'Hara, Frank. LUNCH POEMS
Pacheco, José Emilio. CITY OF MEMORY AND OTHER POEMS
Parenti, Michael. AGAINST EMPIRE
Parenti, Michael. AMERICA BESIEGED
Parenti, Michael. BLACKSHIRTS & REDS
Parenti, Michael. DIRTY TRUTHS
Parenti, Michael. HISTORY AS MYSTERY
Pasolini, Pier Paolo. ROMAN POEMS
Pessoa, Fernando. ALWAYS ASTONISHED
Pessoa, Fernando. POEMS OF FERNANDO PESSOA

Poe, Edgar Allan. THE UNKNOWN POE
Porta, Antonio. KISSES FROM ANOTHER DREAM
Prévert, Jacques. PAROLES
Purdy, James. THE CANDLES OF YOUR EYES
Purdy, James. GARMENTS THE LIVING WEAR
Purdy, James. IN A SHALLOW GRAVE
Purdy, James. OUT WITH THE STARS
Rachlin, Nahid. THE HEART'S DESIRE
Rachlin, Nahid. MARRIED TO A STRANGER
Rachlin, Nahid. VEILS: SHORT STORIES
Reed, Jeremy. DELIRIUM: An Interpretation of Arthur Rimbaud
Reed, Jeremy. RED-HAIRED ANDROID
Rey Rosa, Rodrigo. THE BEGGAR'S KNIFE
Rey Rosa, Rodrigo. DUST ON HER TONGUE
Rigaud, Milo. SECRETS OF VOODOO
Rodríguez, Artemio and Herrera, Juan Felipe. LOTERIA CARDS AND FORTUNE POEMS
Ross, Dorien. RETURNING TO A
Ruy Sánchez, Alberto. MOGADOR
Saadawi, Nawal El. MEMOIRS OF A WOMAN DOCTOR
Sawyer-Lauçanno, Christopher. THE CONTINUAL PILGRIMAGE: American Writers in Paris
        1944-1960
Sawyer-Lauçanno, Christopher, transl. THE DESTRUCTION OF THE JAGUAR
Scholder, Amy, ed. CRITICAL CONDITION: Women on the Edge of Violence
Schelling, Andrew, tr. CANE GROVES OF NARMADA RIVER: Erotic Poems from Old India
Serge, Victor. RESISTANCE
Shepard, Sam. MOTEL CHRONICLES
Shepard, Sam. FOOL FOR LOVE & THE SAD LAMENT OF PECOS BILL
Solnit, Rebecca. SECRET EXHIBITION: Six California Artists
Sussler, Betsy, ed. BOMB: INTERVIEWS
Tabucchi, Antonio. DREAMS OF DREAMS and THE LAST THREE DAYS OF FERNANDO
        PESSOA
Takahashi, Mutsuo. SLEEPING SINNING FALLING
Turyn, Anne, ed. TOP TOP STORIES
Tutuola, Amos. SIMBI & THE SATYR OF THE DARK JUNGLE
Ullman, Ellen. CLOSE TO THE MACHINE: Technophilia and Its Discontents
Valaoritis, Nanos. MY AFTERLIFE GUARANTEED
VandenBroeck, André. BREAKING THROUGH
Vega, Janine Pommy. TRACKING THE SERPENT
Veltri, George. NICE BOY
Waldman, Anne. FAST SPEAKING WOMAN
Wilson, Colin. POETRY AND MYSTICISM
Wilson, Peter Lamborn. PLOUGHING THE CLOUDS
Wilson, Peter Lamborn. SACRED DRIFT
Wynne, John. THE OTHER WORLD
Zamora, Daisy. RIVERBED OF MEMORY